MUSICMANIA

A STARBOOK
SHARON PUBLICATION, INC. CRESSKILL, N.J.

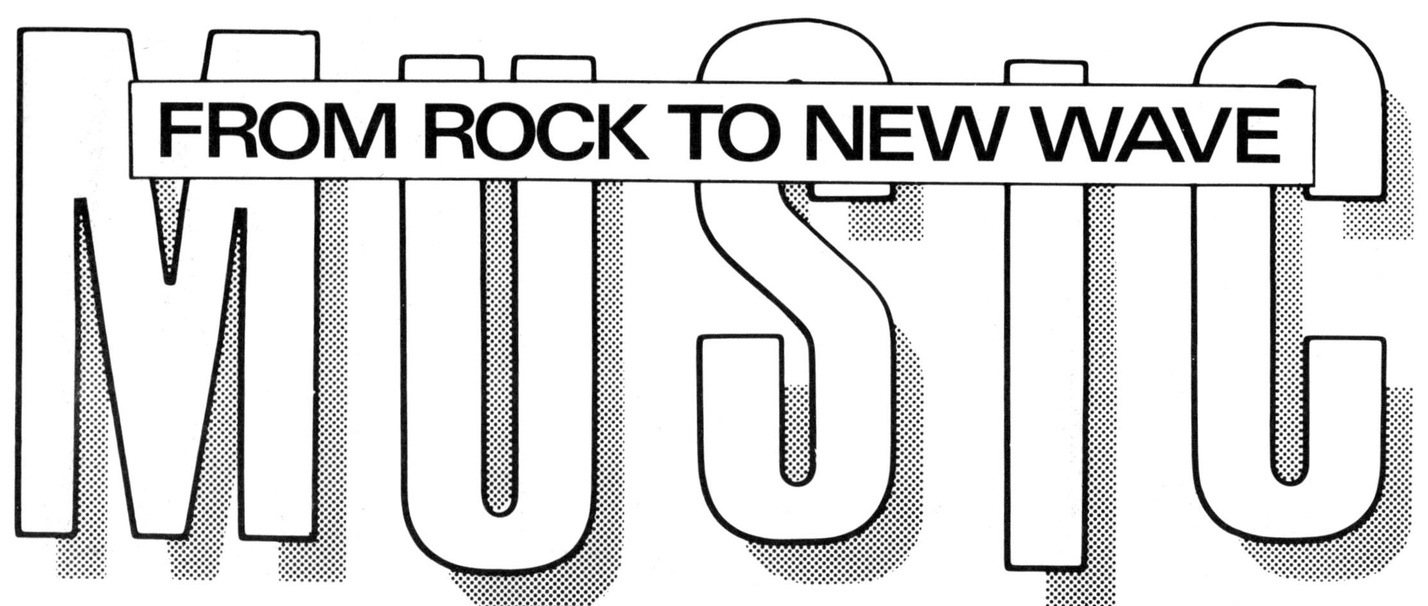

Robyn Flans

I wish to express my deepest gratitude to the Beatles for starting it all inside of me, to the Dirt Band for setting an early positive example, to Gerri for sharing it all with me, to my family for their support, Lynn for his encouragement, Rick for his assistance, Modern Drummer for the opportunities and Vicki, Rochelle and Diane for their ears. To all of those who are a part of me, thank you.

Robyn Flans

This is a STARBOOK.

All correspondence and inquiries should be directed to Sales Dept., Sharon Publications, Inc., 105 Union Avenue, Cresskill, New Jersey 07626.

Sharon Publications Inc. is an Edrei Communications Company

ISBN #0-89531-038-4

Manufactured in the United States of America.

Cover design by: Mike Stromberg
Editor: Mary Jay

CONTENTS

INTRODUCTION

Musicmania is a marvelous collection of two decades of popular music, to relax with, savor and enjoy.

A great deal of us grew up around the time of the Beatles, and many of us from England remember going to that dense dark hole in the wall club called The Cavern, which became the Beatles, second home, as well as the second home of their fans. The walls vibrated with their music, and we all went home dancing on clouds. We have come a long way from those days, and the Beatles have become a legend.

This book concentrates on the groups and artists who have weathered the test of time, and remained in the forefront of the music world.

Space restrictions prohibit the inclusion of many of the artists who have contributed their talents. To them we say we apologize for their absence in this volume, and hope they understand that out of sight is not out of mind.

Mary Jay

The clean-cut appeal of the early Beatles made them acceptable to American parents, but it wasn't long before the mop top four had their locks growing.

One of the first publicity shots

George Harrison

Paul McCar

Ringo Starr

John Lennon

Paul, George and John

CHAPTER ONE

THE BEATLES

When the Beatles appeared on television's *The Ed Sullivan Show* on February 9, 1964, they changed a lot of lives, not only in America but all over the world. The impact made by Paul McCartney, John Lennon, George Harrison and Ringo Starr may be forever impossible to explain, but the fact that they altered the course of music and changed sociological norms from fashion to morals to attitudes cannot be denied. For millions of young people the group became not merely an object of affection, but an emulated and idolized obsession. Musically, the Beatles challenged the field and made experimentation acceptable and desirable, even turning musical emphasis from single rpms to albums. The foursome didn't sound like anyone else who had gone before them, from the R&B of Little Richard to the rockabilly of Elvis Presley —oddly enough two prime influences for the Beatles. Still, there was no one else utilizing the melodies or the harmonies the Beatles produced, no one altered the sound of music as they did and no one band had been self-contained as they were. Previously, music was dominated by a solo artist and back-up musicians, sometimes utilizing grand orchestrations in record production. The Beatles brought with them a raw sound produced by rhythm and lead guitars, a bass and drums.

The group's evolution altered with a few significant personnel changes prior to its fame, and each member enjoyed a variety of musical experiences that led him to that fateful place in time which changed his life.

For 16-year-old John Lennon, 1956 was a significant year. Elvis Presley had such an effect on him he decided he had to have a guitar, and he convinced his mother to buy him one. Since she played banjo, she taught him how to play using banjo chords, and it wasn't long before some schoolmates formed a band, the Quarrymen, named after their school, Quarry Bank.

As a child, James Paul McCartney seemed disinterested in music. He had struggled through a couple of piano lessons and was given an old trumpet by an uncle, but it wasn't until he was 14 that he picked up his first guitar. Like Lennon, he enjoyed music, but it wasn't until Elvis Presley came on the scene that it became a compulsion.

George Harrison, too, had his first guitar at the age of 14. His mother bought him a second-hand instrument and it wasn't long before he taught himself to play competently.

George met Paul shortly after he began attending the Liverpool Institute where Paul was a student. They took the same bus to school each day and became quick friends, spending much of their free time together fooling around with their guitars.

As fate would have it, Paul then met John when a schoolmate, Ivan Vaughan, invited Paul to see the Quarrymen perform. Later, after showing off the fruits of his obsession with the guitar, Paul was asked by John to join the group. Though Paul did introduce John to George, it wasn't until 1958, at least a year later, that George joined the band; thereafter, though various members came and went, the three of them remained the core.

A year previously Lennon had enrolled at art college and there he met a soon-to-be-inseparable friend, Stu Sutcliffe, whom he asked to join the group. Sutcliffe was more interested in art than music but, after watching John, Paul and George rehearse, agreed to join the group (now called Johnny and the Moondogs) as bass guitarist—something the band sorely lacked. Then they seriously began to audition for jobs, calling themselves the Silver Beatles, a name they stuck with throughout 1959. They were still drummerless, but while still the Quarrymen they had met a drummer, Pete Best.

"My mother started a club called the Casbah which was in the basement of our house, and we needed a group to open the club," Pete recalls. "We talked about it and one of the girls we knew said, 'Oh, I know some people,' who turned out to be John, George and Paul. I had seen George previously in a small outfit that had played in a coffee club down the road, so we agreed to meet with them. They came down to the club, looked at the place and were so enthusiastic about it they even helped us decorate.

"Around that time, the vogue was frontline singers," Best explains. "It was a main singer with a backup group behind him, like Elvis Presley, as opposed to the group situation the Beatles popularized where each individual sings. When I first saw the guys perform together, even though they didn't have a drummer, I thought they were great with the harmonies and loved the material they were singing. In 1958, a lot of people were playing middle of the road, top-20 material, but these guys were knocking out songs by Carl Perkins, Chuck Berry and Little Richard and harmonizing like the Everly Brothers. As the Quarrymen, they played at the Casbah for a while, then the next I heard, they had changed their name to the Silver Beatles, auditioned for a big impresario by the name of Larry Parnes and were backing a singer named Jimmy Gentle on a tour of Scotland. For this particular tour," Best continues, "they had a drummer named Tommy Moore, but after Scotland, he'd had enough. That's when I got a call from Paul saying they had an offer to go to Germany and was I interested in joining the group. I went down and auditioned the next day, bashed out about six numbers and that was it. They said, 'Great, you're in,' and two days later, we were in Hamburg."

In 1960, the Silver Beatles played the Indra, a club in Hamburg owned by Bruno Koschmeider, where they performed seven hours a night, seven nights a week for practically nothing, and lived in almost intolerable conditions in back of a cinema. But reaction to the group was good, and finally they were allowed to play Koschmeider's best club, the Kaiserkeller. Around this time they also became known just as the Beatles. The other band on the bill was Rory Storme and the Hurricanes, one of Liverpool's biggest, with Ringo Starr on drums.

"There was heavy competition between my band and the Beatles," says Ringo, "because on the weekends we would play 12 hours a night

between the two bands. At 4:00 or 5:00 in the morning, the Beatles were usually still on, so I'd hang around, and because I was drunk by then, I'd ask them to play soft sentimental songs. They didn't perform much of their own material, but they had a good style. There was a certain appeal about Paul, George and John, though, no offense, I never felt Peter was a great drummer. He had one style, which, I suppose, was fine for them in those days."

As Best remembers it, the group had been offered a job at Hamburg's best club, the Top Ten, and as they prepared to open there, George Harrison's passport was examined, and when it was discovered he was only 17 he was sent home to Liverpool.

"We'd been after Bruno Koschmeider to do certain things and when he didn't, we told him we were going and he said, 'Oh no, you won't,'" Pete explains. "Paul and I went back to his club a few days later to get our stuff and it was pitch black in the place so we lit some matches to get some light. We took our stuff out and continued to play the Top Ten. A couple of days afterwards, we were dragged out by the police and told that we had tried to set fire to Koschmeider's cinema and we had to go home. It was a framing in a way, but once we got home to England we fought the case and we were cleared."

During that trip, however, the Beatles had honed their abilities to a fine art and looked the part as well. Astrid Kirchherr, a woman who befriended the group, and to whom Stu Sutcliffe was engaged, had given them the haircuts that later changed hair fashion. Only Pete Best insisted on keeping his hair the way it had always been, without bangs and combed back. By now, Liverpool had caught on to the sound, however, and in April 1961, the Beatles were invited back to the Top Ten in Germany and stayed several months. Gradually Stu phased himself out of the Beatles, concentrating on art while remaining in Germany with Astrid.

While in Germany, the remaining Beatles backed Tony Sheridan on his recordings of "My Bonnie," "Cry for a Shadow," "Ain't She Sweet" and "When the Saints Go Marching In." They were paid a set fee, there were no contracts, but they were just excited to be recording.

When the Beatles returned to Liverpool in June of 1961, Stuart stayed in Germany. Although John kept in close contact with his best friend, he saw him only once again when Stu and Astrid came to Liverpool seven months later. Tragically, Stu died of a brain hemorrhage just four months later in April 1962.

But in June of 1961 the Beatles created pandemonium in Liverpool. Whereas before, when the Cavern Club had been primarily a jazz club and they had to fight for a booking, the Cavern now became their second home; and it was shortly thereafter that Brian Epstein entered the picture. The Beatles had become stars of sorts and fans sporadically inquired at Epstein's record shop for "My Bonnie" by the Beatles. But because that record actually had been recorded under the name of Tony Sheridan and the Beat Brothers, Epstein had trouble locating it. However, he was persuaded to see the Beatles perform at the Cavern, about 50 yards from his store.

"He liked what he saw and asked to see us in his office," remembers Pete. "He put the decision to us, saying he'd like to become our manager, and he said, 'I have no idea how to manage a group, but I'm a good businessman, and I know records. I'm financially well off and I have a good reputation in Liverpool.' We had wanted someone who could possibly do a little more for us, so in October 1961, Brian Epstein became our manager."

Epstein immediately set out to get the group a recording contract, not an easy task. Decca Records auditioned them and went so far as to record a few tunes, but eventually declined. Following Stu's death, when the Beatles went to play the Star Club in Germany, Brian once again went in pursuit of a contract. EMI's George Martin agreed to audition them and Brian telegraphed the boys in Hamburg.

Upon their return from Germany in June of 1962, the Beatles met with George Martin, and in the following months, Brian received a definite offer. According to some accounts, Martin had decided during the audition that Pete was not good enough to record with the group, but Pete recalls the situation differently.

"The whole thing came out of the blue. We played the Cavern one night and just as I was leaving, Brian asked to see me in his office the next day. I really didn't think anything of it because I had been called into his office numerous times, since I had previously handled the business side of the group and done booking and such. I figured it was to talk about that, but when I went down at 10:00 the next morning, I could tell Brian was agitated and apprehensive. Finally I said, 'Let me have it,' and he turned around and said, 'I've got bad news for you, Pete. The boys want you out and Ringo Starr in.' I was completely shocked and couldn't get my head to work. It just went numb up there. I asked th reason and he told me the boys felt Ringo wa a better drummer. It didn't make sense becaus I was equally as good, if not better. I asked Ringo knew about it and he said it had all bee arranged and Ringo would be joining them o Saturday night. That meant everything had bee taken care of and it had just been left up to Bria to be the hit man for the job. The guys hadn't eve had the decency to be in the office. As far as th reason for it? Well, a lot of people turned aroun and said, 'You weren't aware of it at the time, Pet but you were becoming too popular and wer starting to overshadow the other three.' "

Best met the others on two occasions after tha but no words were exchanged and "from that da to this, I never saw them again," he says.

Ringo Starr, born Richard Starkey, began pla ing drums when he was 13 and hospitalized wit a serious illness that turned into pleurisy. Onc a week a band volunteered to entertain th patients, and Ringo would play around on th group's drums. His affinity for the instrumen continued to grow after his recovery and releas and at 16 he bought a bass drum and made a pa of sticks out of firewood, until his step-fathe bought him a second-hand set for Christma when he was 18. After playing in a few uneven ful musical situations and holding day jobs, h finally decided to become a full-time "profe sional" musician after landing a gig with Ror Storme and the Hurricanes. Ringo was still pla ing with them when Brian called him on a We nesday to ask him to join the Beatles that nigh Not wishing to inconvenience his present ban Ringo suggested Saturday night.

"It was in every newspaper," Ringo recall "Pete had quite a big following and so did I, s there was this whole shouting match. Part of th audience would shout, 'Ringo never, Pete forever and the others would yell, 'Pete never, Ring forever!' But our fans got over it, and the Beatle got busy recording their first record, 'Love Me D One of the reasons they asked Pete to leave wa George Martin, the producer, didn't like Pete drumming, I think, but when I began to play h didn't like me either, so he called in a professiona session man, Andy White."

Martin handed Ringo a tambourine to placat him, and White played the session although, a cording to Ringo, he is the drummer on the albu cut, while White is featured on the single.

"That was the most exciting period of all, thos first couple of records," Ringo smiles. "Every tim it moved into the 50's on the charts, we'd go ou

With the dissolution of the Beatles partnership in 1970, Paul (who had married Linda Eastman in 1969) began a successful solo career which developed into a new group, Wings, in which Linda had an active part. Paul teamed with Stevie Wonder on their hit single "Ebony and Ivory," in 1982, and his Paul McCartney and the All-Star Band (the All Stars being such top names as The Who's Pete Townshend, George Harrison, Nick Lowe and Dave Edmunds, among others who supported Paul for a benefit performance) video is a rarity.

and have dinner and celebrate. When the song hit the 40's, we'd celebrate again. We'd all be waiting in cars or in someone's house for the song to play on the air and then we wouldn't move for three minutes."

"Love Me Do," recorded in August of 1962, was the Number Two song in the U.K. by October. Their follow-up, "Please Please Me," reached the Number One spot in January 1963. ("Please Please Me" in the U.S. in February saw no chart action.) In May the Beatles' first album by the same name was released in the U.K. and stayed at the top position for 30 weeks, only to be replaced by their second album, *With The Beatles*, which held that position for 22 weeks.

In November 1963 the Beatles were selected to play before the Queen, and Brian Epstein set out to discover why America had been so unresponsive to the group. He met with TV variety show host Ed Sullivan, who agreed to book the band for three separate shows, though it took four days for Epstein to convince Sullivan they must receive top billing.

In January 1964 Capitol assumed the role of U.S. distributor from Vee-Jay Records, and "I Want To Hold Your Hand" reached Number One on February 1st, priming America for the Beatles' arrival. On February 7, 1964, they arrived at Kennedy Airport to the welcome of 10,000 screaming fans, and two days later they appeared on *The Ed Sullivan Show*, with a record audience of 73 million. Even the Beatles' idol, Elvis Presley, sent them a congratulatory telegram and there were press conferences, newspaper coverage and complete chaos in New York City. The hearts of American music lovers had been captured!

The following month, John's first book, *In His Own Write*, went straight to the top of the bestseller list, and on the 24th "Can't Buy Me Love" immediately reached the top of both British and American charts. Still in March they began their first film, *A Hard Day's Night*, which was released in August, and the Beatles started their first American tour, breaking attendance records everywhere. A phenomenon had happened—something that had never occurred before and may never be repeated.

1965 saw the Beatles' second feature-film release, *Help*, and their next tour, and in December their *Rubber Soul* LP hit the charts. It was a breakthrough album for them and the world. Until then, critically, they had been considered trendsetters with a flair for pop, but suddenly their albums were taken seriously by music critics and analyzed musically and lyrically. The foursome were regarded as true pioneers and musical geniuses, and albums were by now further apart, due to creative reasons as well as the advent of four-track recording and the technical possibilities with which the group could experiment.

The Beatles' *Yesterday & Today* was released in the summer of '66 to great controversy. A cover they had designed was banned for its crude display of decapitated baby dolls with the Beatles in butchers' outfits. A new album cover was ordered and in some cases, just slapped onto the old.

Right before their summer tour, all hell broke loose with a comment Lennon had made to the *London Evening Standard* newspaper the previous February. It had seemed inconsequential until an American teen magazine, *Datebook*, reprinted the interview and Lennon's comment was featured and magnified. In trying to explain the sociological implications of how music had become so paramount, and wrongly so, he had said, "We're more popular than Jesus now . . ." Misconstrued as Lennon's implying that the Beatles were more popular than Jesus Christ, the comment set off a wave of anti-Beatles demonstrations, Beatle album bonfires and bans on their music.

Brian, worried that John, Paul, George and Ringo were in danger, attempted to cancel the forthcoming tour, but the situation settled itself and the Beatles arrived in America on August 12 for what turned out to be their last tour. Explaining their decision to stop touring, Ringo says, "People just came to scream and shout, which was fine, but after four years, I was becoming such a bad player because I couldn't hear anything. If you look at films, you'll see I'm looking at Paul, John and George's mouths, lip reading where we're up to in a song because I couldn't hear the amps or anything. We were getting real despondent playing live, so we went into the studio for months and months and it got us playing again and experimenting with a lot of avenues."

In August of 1966 *Revolver* was also released, exploring different moods and textures. Harrison, very influenced by the Indian instrument the sitar, had included it on *Rubber Soul*'s "Norwegian Wood," and here it dominated his "Love You To." The album most signified that the group which had once sung "I Want to Hold Your Hand," had finally become obvious individuals with different fancies and directions.

What started out as a concept album never fol-

Although all the Beatles were inspired by Ravi Shankar's sitar, it was George who became an almost fanatic disciple of Indian music studying with the master musician and making use of the sitar on the albums *Rubber Soul* and *Revolver* and later on his solo efforts.

< The Beatles were always at ease during press conferences. John and Paul developed quite a skill at it because of their natural gift for comic retorts.

Λ George first teamed up to play with John and Paul in 1958, though he had previously jammed with Paul since the two had met much earlier.

Right: The films *Help* and *Yellow Submarine* followed *A Hard Day's Night*, but neither was as successful as the Beatles' classic first movie, which inspired the television series *The Monkees* in the late 1960s.

It was Ringo who got the most enjoyment out of acting, whether in the Beatles' films or in other ventures like *The Magic Christian* in the early 70s (with Peter Sellers and Raquel Welch) and an Italian film, *Blind Man*. In *Caveman*, (Right), 1980, he starred with girlfriend Barbara Bach, whom he married in 1983. The couple reteamed in *Princess Daisy*.

lowed through on *Sgt. Pepper's Lonely Hearts Club Band.* It did, however, bring a new Beatles' consciousness to the foreground with its obvious infiltration of drug-related lyrics. No matter how adamantly Lennon insisted a drawing of his son's inspired the title, "Lucy In The Sky With Diamonds" was taken to stand for LSD. "A Day In The Life" was banned from BBC for references made to a man who "blew his mind out in a car" and the words "4,000 Holes In Blackburn, Lancashire" were taken to refer to needle marks. Needle marks were also assumed to be the subject of "Fixing A Hole," and Ringo's "With A Little Help From My Friends" voiced "getting high."

Just before the release of the album, Paul's admission that he had taken LSD appeared in *Life Magazine*, creating a stir. Brian Epstein joined John and George in admitting he had also taken the drug, but in time that commotion also died down. Shortly after that, Brian died of an accidental overdose of drugs he was reportedly taking to help him sleep.

Magical Mystery Tour, an hour color TV show, was the Beatles' next venture, and the first that was not successful. The American TV deal was actually cancelled on the basis of the British showing.

In May 1968 the Beatles began work on *The Beatles*, known as the White Album, and Ringo says that on one level this album made the group more unified.

"On *Pepper* we were like session players, using all those orchestras and sound effects. It was good fun, but I felt like we were back to being a self-contained group on the White Album."

Perhaps instrumentally; but musically the forces had become polarized—Paul with his tuneful "Martha My Dear" and "Blackbird," and John with his "Happiness Is A Warm Gun" and "Glass Onion." They went in even further directions when John married his second wife, Yoko Ono, forming with her the Plastic Ono Band. Paul released a solo album the following year in 1970, even though the group's 1969 album *Abbey Road* was an attempt at solidifying the unit once more.

"The breakup came because everyone had ideas of what *he* wanted to do, whereas everyone used to have ideas of what *we* wanted to do as a group," Ringo explains. "We weren't really fulfilling John's musical ambitions, or Paul's or George's, or my own in the end, because it was separate. You could see it coming, but like everything else, we held off for a while. Then it just got too silly and we had a meeting about what everyone wanted to do."

The result was the dissolution of the partnership and while each went on to do separate projects, none came even close to the magnitude or creativity or excitement that occurred while the Beatles were a unit. After only six years in the public eye, they managed to change the course of music, becoming catalysts for what music began around them and at the root of much of the music we hear today.

Perhaps Paul McCartney has managed to stay involved with music on the most consistent level with his band, Wings, and various other projects. George and Ringo have continued to record solo projects and Ringo has acted in several films. John and Yoko's Plastic Ono Band enjoyed some success, and just following his reemergence from a quasi-retirement, John was shot and killed outside his New York apartment on December 8, 1980.

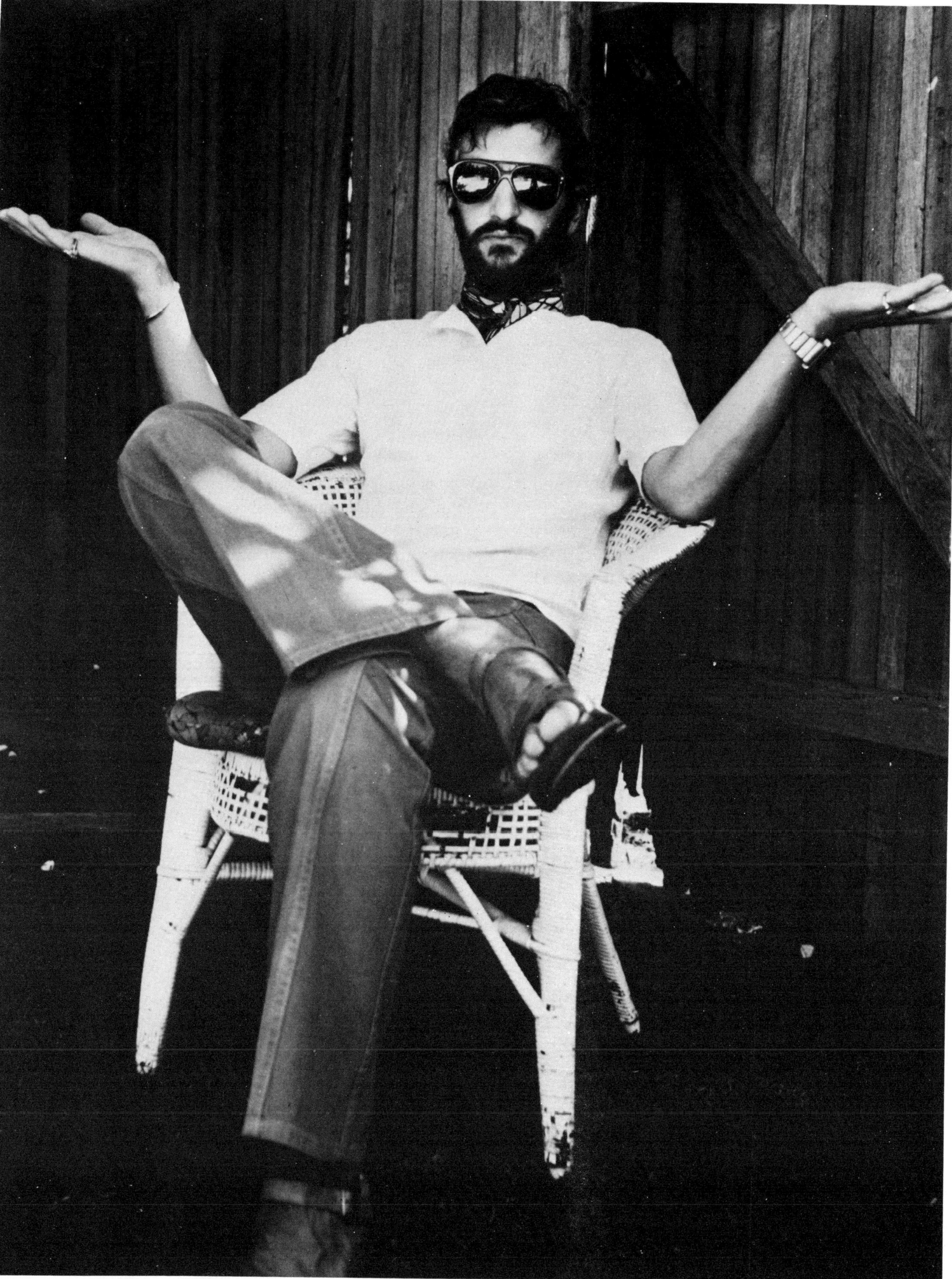

THE ROLLING STONES

CHAPTER TWO

When the Rolling Stones entered the picture in 1963, it was as if two factions were pitted against one another—the Beatles vs. the Stones. Very rarely did someone love both, and, at best, one had a vague appreciation for his or her least favorite of the two. More often the feelings were even more polarized. Although the Beatles seemed radical when they first came onto the English scene with their long hair and leather jackets, they soon became England's good boys, while the Stones were the bad boys, musically and in attitude. Their devil-may-care impression stirred a large part of the masses as much as their more raw, gruff music and their drug- and sex-related lyrics. While one of the Beatles' first recorded tunes was "I Want To Hold Your Hand," one of the Stones' earliest recordings was "I Just Want To Make Love To You," and while the Beatles eventually won the hearts of parents, children were forbidden to enjoy or emulate the Stones. Of course, to many, that made the appeal that much greater.

The long saga of the Rolling Stones began in 1960 when Mick Jagger and Keith Richards ran into one another on a train. Keith was going to art school and Mick was on his way to the London School of Economics with a stack of albums under his arm. Keith was amazed that there was someone else in the world with the same musical tastes, especially considering they had to send away to Chicago's Chess Records to obtain such prize possessions as recordings by Chuck Berry, Little Walter and Muddy Waters. They had known each other years back as youngsters, and now the common denominator renewed their friendship. Keith invited Mick over and they began exchanging musical ideas. Keith hadn't been playing guitar long, nor had Mick been singing long, but they got together at a mutual friend's house with a couple of others, and shared their crude talents.

It was 1962 when they discovered the Ealing Club and Alexis Korner and Cyril Davies. Since 1960 Korner's group had been the first in England to play rhythm and blues. The first night they went, Alexis announced a guest guitarist, none other than Brian Jones, playing bar slide guitar. An association began, and soon Brian, already a professional in the eyes of Keith and Mick, who were amateurs, decided to become involved with them instead of another band with which he was already rehearsing. Mick's, Keith's and Brian's first performance as a unit was a result of Alexis, who was unable to make his scheduled appearance at the Marquee Club.

Then the search for a drummer and a bass player began. Tony Chapman initially became the Stones' drummer until the members realized they weren't satisfied with him. Chapman did, however, recommend a bass player by the name of Bill Wyman who knew how to play and had already been in rock bands for three years.

Drummer Charlie Watts recalls that he was with Alexis Korner's Blues Incorporated for a year, but his main gig was as a designer. "After the year, I gave up my chair to Ginger Baker (later of Cream) because I thought he was a better drummer than I was," Charlie tells. "I played with three other bands and then I was asked to join Mick and the other three. I lived with them, and since I was between jobs as a designer, I used to leave their apartment and go for interviews while I was playing with them. After six months, though, I saw I was making more money playing than I could make as a designer. Suddenly I was a professional musician, whatever that is, and I had to join the union."

When Charlie joined it all came together, and in February 1963 the Stones got their big break. Giorgio Gomelsky called them to play his club, the Crawdaddy, when the scheduled band didn't show. After just a few weeks, the Stones, then a six-piece with Ian Stewart on piano, became London's sensation. When the Beatles, particularly, endorsed the Stones by going to the Crawdaddy, everybody who was anybody had to go. In March, Andrew Oldham, a Beatles' press agent, was coerced by a journalist to see the Stones. He was immediately impressed with the group and decided it wouldn't be long before the public would need a band opposing the Beatles. In May the Stones signed a management agreement with Oldham and the agent with whom he was sharing space, Eric Easton. A week later Andrew took the band into the studio and produced Chuck Berry's "Come On." It wasn't the R&B they loved, because the record was aimed at commerciality, but when released in early June it bolted into the top 30.

Interestingly enough, Andrew Oldham tried to change the Stones' scruffy image. They even

Above Right: Mick celebrated his 32nd birthday at a sellout concert at Indiana University on July 26, 1975. Even today the Stones lead singer gives an upbeat, exciting and energetic performance that belies his years. Right: The Stones 1978 U.S. tour was eagerly awaited with anticipation by fans and proved that the group still had what it takes.

appeared on *Thank Your Lucky Stars*, one of England's most popular music shows, in uniform checkered jackets, but soon discarded the conformity for their own desired attire. Their own chosen clothing proved to be an advantage, though, for their sloppy appearance more often than not got them press.

On September 29 the Stones began their first big European tour with Bo Diddley and the Everly Brothers, and consequently dropped all Diddley tunes from their show.

The next single they recorded, oddly enough, was a Lennon/McCartney tune, "I Wanna Be Your Man." The two versions of the song are as different as night and day, but it was the Stones' first big hit and the Beatles' version had not been released yet.

1964 was the Stones' big year. In January they released an EP (4 tracks) and at the end of the month began their first album, *The Rolling Stones*, released in April. The EP was still in the top 20 when the album hit the top 10.

By the beginning of February the kind of riots and mania the Beatles had been experiencing hit the Stones on their second European tour. Once again, in May, they embarked on yet a third European tour and shy Charlie remembers: "The worst time in my life was about the time the Rolling Stones became like the Beatles. There were girls screaming and carrying on and I couldn't stand it. I loved it for what it meant and what the band was doing, but I couldn't stand not being able to do anything. I hated it."

But while England experienced Stonemania, their first U.S. single, "Not Fade Away," only went as far as Number 48 on the American charts. Their arrival at Kennedy Airport was far from that of the Beatles' first welcome. No one had come to greet them. They performed *The Les Crane Show* and the next morning flew to Los Angeles to tape *The Hollywood Palace*. For the group, however, the highlight of their American trip was recording at Chess Studios in Chicago, the studio of their idols. It was a great thrill for them when many of their heroes dropped by the Stones' sessions, including Muddy Waters, whose song "Rollin' Stone" inspired the group's name. They even had the same engineer who had worked with Chuck Berry, Howlin' Wolf and Bo Diddley. The group cut nine tracks and released one as their next single, "It's All Over Now," which went straight to the top of Britain's top 10. Released in the States, it finally made it as high as Number 25.

Their first U.S. stop was San Bernardino, California, where they were met by a receptive crowd.

But it went downhill from there, and in many places in the U.S. the Stones were fortunate to attract 600 people in a 15,000-seat hall. They returned home, however, to pandemonium at their own airport and the European tour exhibited the same.

By their second American tour, in October 1964, they still had not had a Number One hit, but the fans had gathered and the insanity had finally spread to the United States.

The Stones' first two U.S. albums, *The Rolling Stones* and *12x5*, released mid and late 1964, did poorly initially, although their third album, *Now,* released in May 1965, did better, and finally their fourth album, *Out of Our Heads*, proved a success. The single "Satisfaction" was their first Number One hit, and finally the group was on its way. In 1966, *December's Children* and *Big Hits* made the top of the charts and *Aftermath* reached the Number Two position. From then on, the rest of their albums all reached the top of the charts throughout their ongoing career.

By the beginning of 1967, however, personal problems began to interfere. Drug busts were constant, and Brian Jones was certain his three were frame-ups. Entire books have been written on the Rolling Stones, their chaotic personal relationships and the supposed power struggle between Mick and Brian for leadership status. Brian ended up in the hospital twice that year for nervous breakdowns, and the following year he became even more fragile with continued police harassment. It had definitely begun to affect his creative talents. While he had earlier integrated such unusual instruments as the dulcimer, marimbas and sitar (beginning with *Aftermath*), he was barely even showing up to sessions anymore. It all happened so quickly that the public hadn't even become aware he had left the group when, in June, the tragic news of his death reached the airwaves. He drowned in his swimming pool on July 3, 1969. An autopsy showed the death was drug related.

Mick Taylor (previously of John Mayall's group) had already been contacted to join the Stones' upcoming tour prior to Brian's death. The Stones' flirtation with the demonic, however, on such albums as *Their Satanic Majesties Request,* known as their psychedelic offering, and *Beggar's Banquet,* culminated that tour in one of rock's most tragic events. The Stones had decided to do a free concert in the San Francisco area at Altamont Race Track on December 6. According to accounts, the crowd was restless, waiting for the Stones to perform, and the result was a stabbing of a young boy by the Hell's Angels, hired as security guards by the Stones. The film *Gimme Shelter* chronicles the events.

Although certainly Altamont has been rehashed and rehashed, it never damaged the band's career. *Sticky Fingers*, the album released after that tour, surely did not suffer, nor did *Exile On Main Street*, released at the time of their 1972 tour.

In 1975 Mick Taylor exited and Ron Wood (ex-Faces member) joined, and finally, in 1978, the release of their *Some Girls* album marked their return to their R&B roots, which expanded in their *Tattoo You* album.

Having come full circle with exalted product and fame, today the Stones are considered the greatest rock and roll band in the world. If nothing else, their longevity continues to be admired since they are the oldest rock and roll group to remain intact. Although they enjoy outside projects during the months away from co-members, when they come together to record on tour the world isn't any less interested in seeing their concerts or hearing their albums. The anticipation of their next step is always met with great expectation and pleasure.

Brian Jones, who formed the Rolling Stones with Keith and Mick in 1962, was rhythm guitarist for the group until his death in 1969.

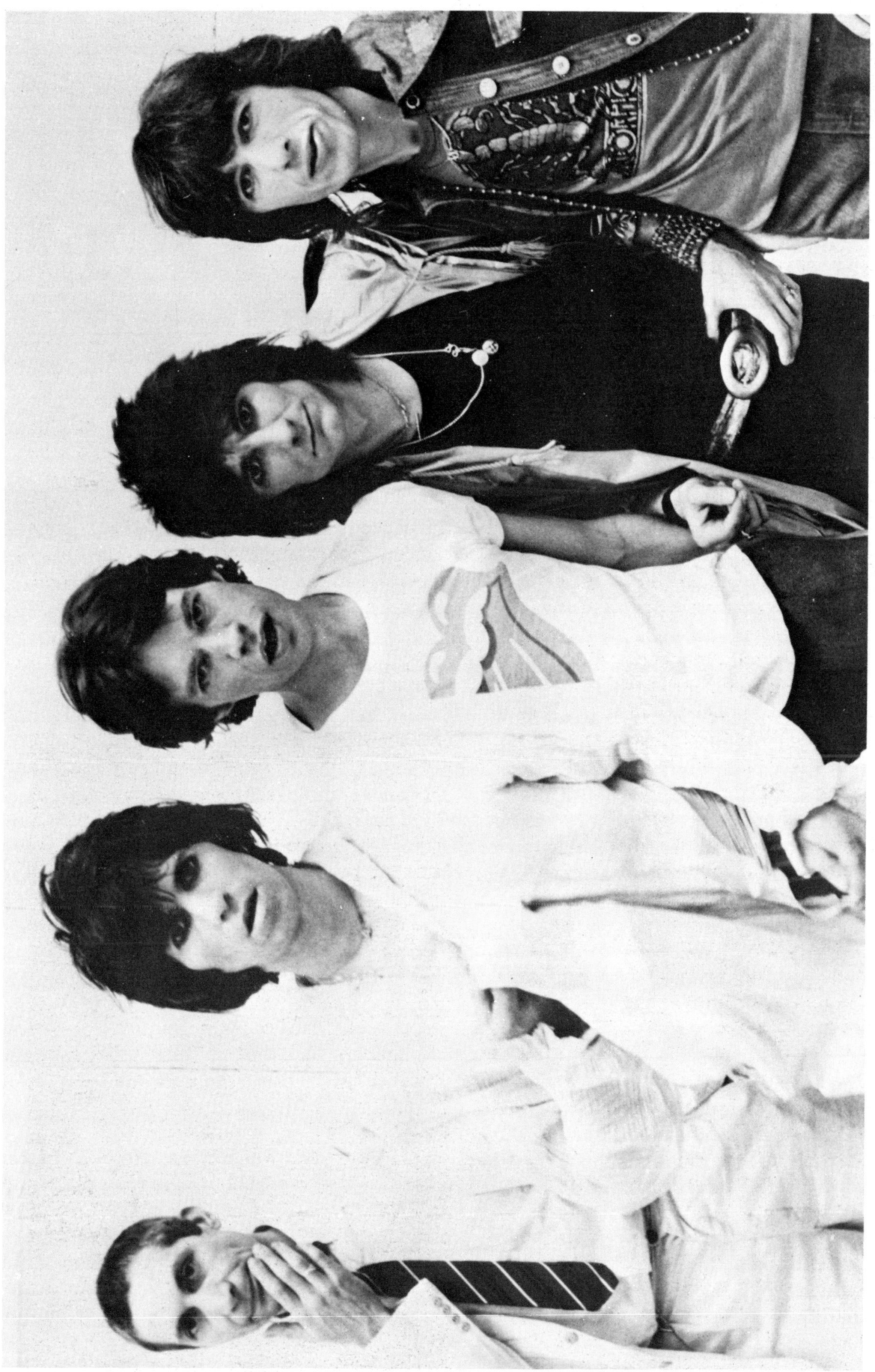

CHAPTER THREE

THE WHO

Pete Townshend and John Entwhistle were only 14 when they formed their first group. The Confederates, however, never got further than rehearsal before Entwhistle began devoting time to another band. Finally, a year later, they formed still another band called the Scorpions, but that hardly got off the ground before John ran into Roger Daltrey, a student at the same school. It was 1960 when Daltrey invited John to audition for *his* band, The Detours, which was actually playing gigs. John finally convinced Pete to join as well, and after going through a couple of lead singers, Roger assumed that role and Pete changed from rhythm to lead guitarist. As a four-piece, they decided the name The Who had a quirky ring to it, and thus The Who was born.

Soon, however, the band found itself drummerless and a search ensued. One night, while the group was using a session player on a gig, Keith Moon appeared out of nowhere, demanding to play with the band. He sat in with them and once the three musicians heard the power with which he propelled them, they asked him to join immediately. He left the Beachcombers, a surf band with whom he had been playing, and the foursome was intact.

About that time Helmut Gorden, whose hobby was managing the band, welcomed publicist Pete Meaden into the fold, hoping some knowledge about the music business might rub off on him. Meaden largely became responsible for creating the group's image in his own, so to speak, since he was quite enamoured with the Mod movement in England. He put them into mod clothes from exclusive Carnaby Street, and even changed their name to the High Numbers, a name more suitable for the Mod Society.

More important, though, was that this newfound identity created an excitement within the band, and a direction and a goal. The style created an attitude in the group members, which in turn, created an atmosphere. They had always played R&B, but now there were mannerisms and movements they adopted to complete the picture.

Meaden arranged their first recording date, at which they did "I'm the Face," "Zoot Suit" and "Here T'is," records that never made it. About that time the group realized how ineffectual its present management was! Gordon didn't really know the business, and Meaden didn't know how to put his knowledge to work.

Kit Lambert and Chris Stamp entered the picture. They were looking for a band to use in a film, but when they saw the realities of the band's management situation, suggested they take over in that capacity. Since the boys had been underage, Helmut Gorden's contract proved invalid, so the legalities were simple enough.

While playing at the Railway Hotel one night, as fate would have it, Townshend's guitar neck broke off on the exceptionally low ceiling. A girl in the front row, laughing at the incident, so infuriated Pete that he took the remains of his guitar and smashed it to bits. By the group's next performance the crowd eagerly was awaiting that grand finale and an act had been born.

Already, though, Pete had adopted other bits into his showmanship. His trademark windmill-like sweep of his guitar was born one night when,

From Left: Roger Daltrey, Pete Townshend, John Entwhistle and Keith Moon.

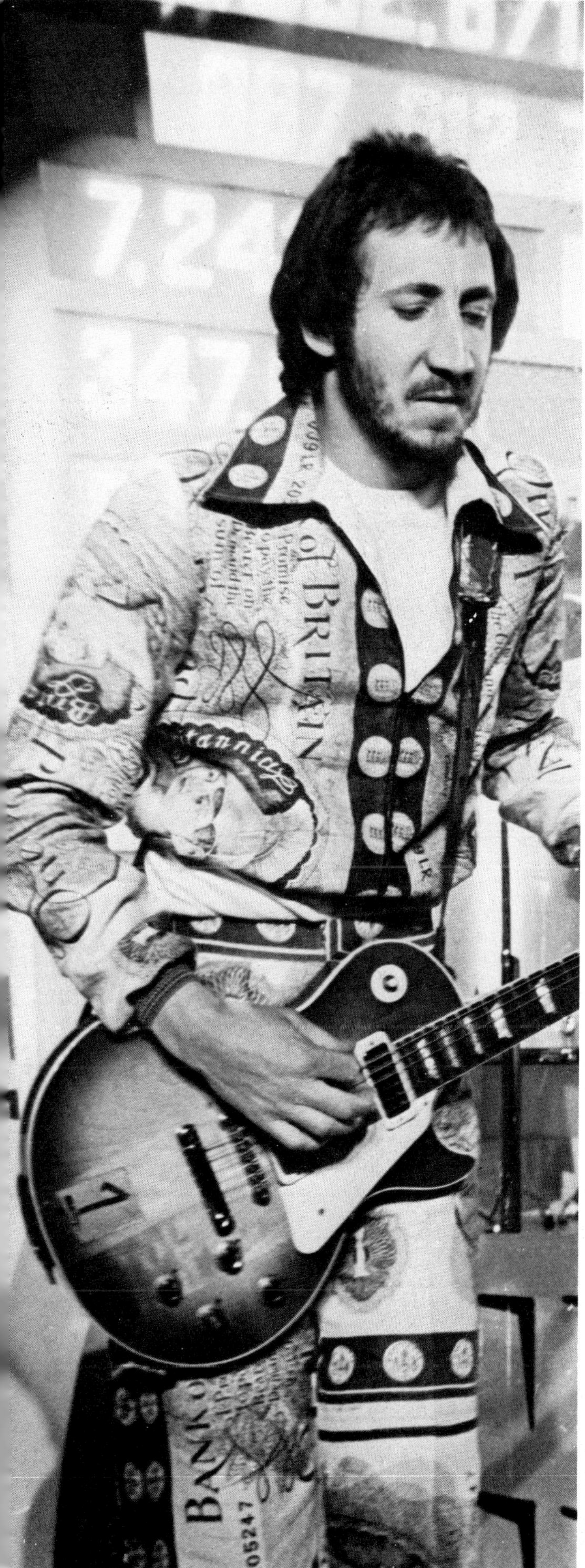

while standing in the wings, he spotted Keith Richards inadvertently making a similar movement. Townshend's usage of feedback in the music also became a signature sound when he decided the accidental feedback was appealing to him, and it added to the already powerhouse drums and wailing vocals. They had become the ultimate Mod band and soon reverted back to the name of The Who. It was Kit Lambert who decided to add the words "maximum R&B" to fill their posters and make them look more impressive. That's how they were known by the time they became the resident Tuesday night group at the influential Marquee Club.

When Pete wrote and demoed "I Can't Explain," the Kinks' record producer, Shel Talmy, got involved and a deal was secured with Decca for both British and American distribution. "Bald Headed Woman" was the B side (with Jimmy Page on fuzz guitar), released in January 1965. The record sold well amongst the accumulated fans, but didn't even enter the charts. With other group appearances on all of the main TV music shows, however, it finally did reach the Number 10 position. (It only reached Number 93 in the U.S.) Their next single, "Anyhow, Anyway, Anywhere," only reached Number 13, but they were quickly becoming the topic of conversation and hailed as the most original new band around.

Pete's next composition met with a lot of resistance in the band, particularly from Roger who felt they had strayed too far from their R&B roots. A variety of arguments were to be the norm, however, throughout their career. "My Generation" reached Number 3 on the charts, and when released in America went to Number 74. But the song became an anthem for the struggling youth of the 1960s and embodied the qualities for which The Who's songs and attitude would become known—rebellion, defiance and a fight against the frustration of suppression.

Their first album, *My Generation*, was released at the end of 1965, did extremely well, and they embarked on their first European tour. Upon their return, however, management realized they wanted to break ties with producer Talmy since The Who needed more creative control in the studio. Talmy ended up getting a percentage of their music for years to come, but at least they were free of him creatively and Pete was able to produce their next single on Robert Stigwood's new label, Reaction. They tried to get out of their U.S. Decca deal as well, since the company was conventional and stodgy, but to no avail. Decca in England released "The Kids Are Alright" off the *My Generation* album, but two weeks later Reaction released "I'm A Boy," which became their first Number One hit in England. Decca tried only once more to cash in on their former act's success by releasing "La La La Lies" which only reached Number 45. It was the same time The Who's second album, and first on Reaction, came out. *A Quick One* reached fourth position on the charts and included a 10-minute mini-opera called "A Quick One While He's Away" and their next single, "Happy Jack."

The Who still had not infiltrated the U.S. and their albums, released many months after those in England, went fairly unnoticed. They were invited, however, to join the *Murray The K Show* in New York, which performed six shows a day, seven days a week, and when The Who continued their instrument-breaking ritual, they became an instant success with audiences. When the single "Happy Jack" was released in the U.S., Decca hired additional promotion people and the song reached 28 on the U.S. charts. It began the love affair between The Who and America that would continue to flourish with time.

The band returned home to the success of their next single, "Pictures Of Lily," and began a furious tour of Europe before returning to the States in June 1967 for the historic Monterey Pop Festival—where America was finally made aware of this awesome band. After the festival they went on a seven-week tour with Herman's Hermits, an odd coupling that made for some frustration on the part of The Who. It was on this first U.S. tour that their hotel-smashing reputation began (which really was Keith Moon's delight), subsequently banning them from a variety of hotels across the country.

"I Can See For Miles," their next single, went as high as Number 9 on the U.S. charts and their next album, *The Who Sell Out*, was critically acclaimed. Suggesting a pop art motif, something acquired from Pete's art school days, the album, complete with jingles and commercials, only reached into the top 50's in America. The album also sported one of the most outrageous covers for that time, with Roger seated in a bathtub covered with baked beans.

Returning to the U.S. in 1968, The Who once again reverted to the instrument breakings which they had pretty much phased out with English fans. Since it had managed to captivate those audiences, they felt it might be their hook into the Amerian crowds as well, and even though it was an extremely expensive way to make a

Keith's erratic personality had him constantly walking the fine line between clown and maniac, but friends say that before Keith's death in 1978, he was seriously working at kicking his drug and drinking habits.

point, their live shows have always been crucial. Once they stopped the actual demolition, however, they had somehow learned to maintain that energy and keep the aggression intact, making a Who concert an explosive event either way.

A landmark project in 1969, *Tommy* is considered the first successful rock opera. The project, which turned into a double album, also seemed to unify the members in one common goal. Incredibly successful, The Who began to perform *Tommy* on the road, with Roger, as the lead singer and focal point of the band, giving them a strong identity. There was a maturation in their performance, a certain raw sophistication that other groups had not been able to put across. Even Europe's opera houses agreed to book the show, followed by New York's Metropolitan Opera House. A year after it was released the LP was rereleased, reaching Number 4. That summer, *Live At Leeds* was also released, hailed as one of the finest live albums in rock history.

Tommy, however, became the beginning of the end for The Who's relationship with Kit Lambert. Lambert had produced all their albums since Shel Talmy had been ousted, and the band had become increasingly interested in improving its sound. Although Lambert had been a mastermind for ideas, he lacked musical techniques. Glyn Johns, who had engineered some of The Who albums, produced their next album, *Who's Next,* which reached Number 4 in the U.S. in 1971, supported by an extremely successful tour.

A stage production of *Tommy* followed, and then the purchase of their own studio, Ramport. Pete was writing material for *Quadrophenia,* a story about growing up in the early '60s as seen through the eyes of a young mod. Meanwhile, Pete having already completed a solo album, Roger released his first solo album, which was followed by John's releasing his third.

Although the critics raved about *Quadrophenia,* it didn't do terribly well on the charts and presented great technical difficulties in attempting its live reproduction.

Pete didn't particularly want to get too involved with the filming of *Tommy;* in his heart the project was a part of his past, though in the end he became its musical director. Directed by Ken Russell, the film was a major box-office success on both sides of the Atlantic.

It was about this time that Kit Lambert and Chris Stamp were officially released and Bill Curbishley, who had managed Roger's solo venture, became The Who's new manager (although not officially until March 1976). The band would have recorded a new album considerably sooner if Roger hadn't accepted the lead in Ken Russell's next film, *Liztomania.* Instead, John took his group, Ox, on tour and Pete began work on his new solo album.

In 1975 both *Tommy* and *Liztomania* were released, Daltrey released his second solo album and *The Who By Numbers* came out accompanied by open warfare between Pete and Roger in separate interviews. A tour followed, however, and they were in fine form, raking in superlative reviews.

In 1977, Daltrey released another solo album, as did Pete, and they set about to begin their next album. But Keith Moon had become a problem. On the last tour there had been nights where he could barely play, and now in the studio his drumming began to suffer in its consistency. His drinking had gotten out of hand, as had Pete's and John's, but Keith had always had that erratic personality, the tendency toward the insane, constantly walking the fine line between clown and maniac. The album was slow in the making and they even lost their producer, Glyn Johns. When Pete finally confronted Moon, presenting an ultimatum, the drummer shaped up quickly and made the attempt to clean up his act. Keith Moon had been honestly working at kicking his drug and drinking habits; he lost weight, and he intended to marry his long-time fiance, when he died on September 7, 1978. The world not only lost a great drummer, but rock's most lovable personality. Shortly after Moon's death, "The Kids Are Alright" was released and remains a testament to the group and a tribute to Moon.

Now a decision had to be made. Prior to Keith's death, The Who had been the longest surviving *intact* rock and roll band. Could they keep going? Did they want to? Could they replace the beloved Keith Moon? Did they want to? If they were going to continue as a band, did they want to tour at all? Roger felt the band should use different session drummers for their various projects and Pete suggested changing the name and adding perhaps *three* new musicians. They finally decided to carry on with The Who with Kenney Jones, a founding member of the now defunct Small Faces, perhaps the only other important Mod band in music history.

"I was with Keith the night before he died," Kenney recalls. "We went to the premiere of a Buddy Holly film which was Paul McCartney's film. There was a reception and we were talking with Paul and he said, 'I've got this idea and I want to call it *Rockestra* where I'll get a lot of

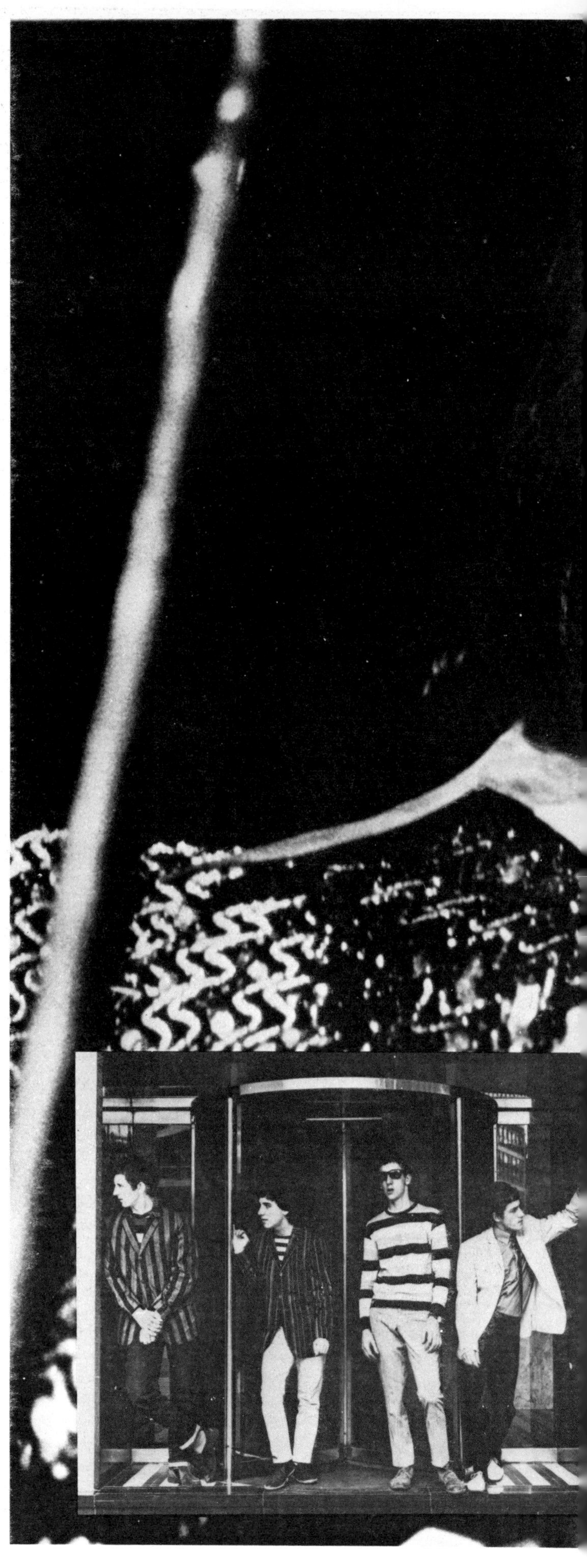

Right: In 1978, drummer Kenney Jones (top right) replaced Keith Moon and helped revive the grop until 1982, when they put the act on hold. Pete had decided he didn't want to tour anymore, but The Who jokingly say the band is not splitting up and will continue to record as a group.

musicians together. I want you, Kenney, Keith and John Bonham (Led Zeppelin) with all these other guitarists, Pete Townshend and Eric Clapton.' Keith and I were enjoying each other's company and when we left, we decided the idea was fantastic. The next day I woke up and he didn't."

It wasn't long after that Bill Curbishley phoned Jones, asking him to join the band as an equal member. He met with Pete the next day and at the end of the meeting, he was thinking to himself, "Jesus, I've *got* to join the band. It's how I grew up, it's a part of me, I know them and it's what I stand for."

Kenney Jones revived The Who, and Townshend openly said that with Keith's death came the death of the old Who. And Kenney handled it beautifully. From the start, through *Face Dances* and *It's Hard* to the live performances of two tours, he had no desire to become the next Keith Moon, a wise choice on his part. He never had to live up to Moon's shadow, for he is simply a different drummer, a strong and stable foundation, and he was accepted on his own abilities.

Jones had a week in which to learn about thirty songs before his first gig in France in front of 8,000 people, and to play at Wembley in front of 100,000 people the following week. The next year, however, was Kenney's first actual tour, for which the band added John "Rabbit" Bundrick to perform auxiliary keyboards. It turned into a tragic tour. On December 3, 1979, 11 fans were crushed to death trying to get into the auditorium at a Cincinnati concert. It was rock's most senseless and irresponsible event. The concert had been festival seating (first come, first served) and it was not The Who's fault that security had been lax. The band wasn't even aware of what had happened until they came off stage after their concert.

Pete had been drinking increasingly more heavily, and by the next Who tour, even though he had quit drinking, he finally announced he no longer wanted to go on the road. He had been talking about that feeling since 1978, actually, but now he was firm. Although it was not a decision shared by the rest of the group, in 1982 they did their farewell tour, much to the disappointment of their fans. It appears, however, that they will continue to record as a group, and half-jokingly and half-seriously Kenney comments, "The band is not splitting up. It's definitely the last long tour, but maybe we'll do a short tour." He laughed. "The Who's last *short* tour."

CHAPTER FOUR

By 1964, Eric Burdon and the Animals were filling the airwaves with gutsy sounds. The Animals, as the group became known, had several hits before Eric decided to go it alone. 1983 saw the re-emergence of The Animals intact with a new LP, *Ark*, and a successful nationwide tour.

Although Peter and Gordon stayed a duo until the end of the '60s, their final hit was "Lady Godiva" in 1966. Today Peter Asher produces acts like Linda Ronstadt and James Taylor.

THE SIXTIES

The British Invasion

There had never been a more exciting time, musically, than the '60s. The Beatles had begun a movement which resulted in a complete change. The change created hundreds of new bands on both sides of the Atlantic. The '50s had spawned a few top artists, but nothing close to the number of groups that hit in the '60s. Not even when the new wave movement occurred in the late '70s, did it create an entire altercation or springboard. It was all new back then and there seemed to be no confines once the Beatles had broken down those barriers.

It would be presumptuous to say, however, that the Beatles created it all, for such movements as the folk-rock era had begun long ago with folk. The Beatles only helped influence a more sophisticated outpouring. But even Bob Dylan has said that the Beatles changed his life.

The Motown era, of course, had already been born from R&B, was around far longer than the Beatles, but that R&B sound was put into a new context once the Beatles emerged.

The business was new as well. Because of the sudden success of these four moptops, little independent record companies sprang up all over the place, and they were willing to take chances. Since the public had grown accustomed to welcoming a new band, it behooved the record companies to bring as much product as possible to the masses. Certainly the economics were such that it was easier to put a band on the road, and cheaper to record on four-track than 24-track, but in those days, taking chances was the precedent set by the Beatles, and both record companies and audiences benefited.

PETER AND GORDON

Peter Asher and Gordon Waller teamed up in 1962 and signed with EMI (Capitol in the U.S.) near the beginning of 1964. It was to their fortune that Paul McCartney was then dating Peter's sister, Jane, for the previously unrecorded Lennon/McCartney "World Without Love" made Peter and Gordon's debut album a smash. In 1966 McCartney, curious as to whether it was his name or his talent that provided a hit, penned "Woman" under the pseudonym Bernard Webb, and once again Peter and Gordon had a hit. "Lady Godiva" was one of their final hits in 1966 until the team broke up in the latter '60s. Asher took a job as managing director at the Beatles label, Apple, and signed a new artist by the name of James Taylor. Taylor's debut album didn't attract any attention, but Asher became his manager and moved to the U.S., where today he still produces James Taylor and such other artists as Linda Ronstadt and Bonnie Raitt.

CHAD AND JEREMY

Like Peter and Gordon, Chad and Jeremy's pop sound was more successful in the U.S. than their native country.

Chad Stuart and Jeremy Clyde met at the Central School of Drama, naturally gravitating towards one another since both played guitars. Their first hit, "Yesterday's Gone," was in 1964, followed by "Summer Song" and "Willow Weep For Me." Known for a more orchestrated folk-pop sound, the duo broke up in 1967 soon after releasing the highly acclaimed *Cabbages And Kings* LP, considered quite progressive for its time. Jeremy had left once before to continue his acting, but had returned. This time, however, he retired from music altogether and the split was permanent.

GERRY AND THE PACEMAKERS

By the time the Beatles had moved to the top in England, Gerry and the Pacemakers were not far behind.

Gerry Marsden, Freddy Marsden, Leslie Maguire and Les Chadwick started in the cellar clubs of Liverpool, alternating with the Beatles at the famed Cavern. The group was managed with the magical touch of Brian Epstein, who was convinced that had not the Beatles been born Gerry and the Pacemakers would have been the biggest stars. When the Beatles refused a tune called "How Do You Do It?" the group grabbed it and it reached Number 9 on American charts in August 1964. Between 1963 and 1966 the group had several hits, most notably "Don't Let The Sun Catch You Crying" (summer '64) and "Ferry Cross The Mersey" (February '65).

DAVE CLARK FIVE

This group was almost accidentally formed when members of the Tottenham Hotspurs, an amateur soccer team, needed money to get to Holland to play a Dutch team in 1962. Dave Clark put a band together to play dances to raise the fare. Mike Smith, Rick Huxley, Lenny Davidson and Dennis Peyton all played instruments. Clark did not, but when they needed a drummer, his choice of instruments was made for him.

One of the only bands with a drummer/leader, the Dave Clark Five had seven hits in 1964, including the most memorable "Glad All Over," "Bits And Pieces" and "Any Way You Want It." They were the second group to perform on the prestigious *The Ed Sullivan Show* and actually the first English group to tour America in the spring of 1964 when the Beatles held off until summertime.

HERMAN'S HERMITS

By the time he was 14, Peter Noone had started Herman's Hermits. When Noone was 16, the band was already a local success in Northern England (Manchester), complete with a fan club. They pursued producer Mickie Most by playing a series of gigs and sending him a prepaid ticket and a night in Manchester's biggest hotel in order to get him to see the band. Most revamped the band, including Karl Green and Keith Hopwood and adding Derek Leckenby and Barry Whitwam, obtained a record deal and the band had one hit after another. Their top songs included "Can't You Hear My Heartbeat" ('65), "Silhouettes" ('65), "Mrs. Brown, You've Got A Lovely Daughter" ('65), "Wonderful World" ('65), and "There's A Kind Of A Hush" ('67).

THE HOLLIES

After several personnel changes, the Hollies scored with a few significant hits in the mid '60s, including "Bus Stop" ('66), "Stop, Stop, Stop" ('66), "On A Carousel" ('67) and "Carrie Anne" ('67). Perhaps the most important figure to emerge from this group was Graham Nash, who departed late '68 and went on to bigger and better things. The Hollies did score, however, with a major hit in 1969, "He Ain't Heavy, He's My Brother," and recently had another hit with a cover of "Stop In The Name Of Love."

In contrast to the melodic pop sounds of the aforementioned groups, just as the Stones' music rivaled that of the Beatles', the following bands followed more closely to the Stones' gritty, blues-flavored, sometimes discordant sound.

THE ANIMALS

As early as 1963, Eric Burdon, Alan Price, John Steel, Hilton Valentine and Bryan "Chas" Chandler (who later discovered Jimi Hendrix and became his first manager) were working under the name of the Alan Price combo. Their act was so wild, they eventually changed their name to the Animals. Led by Burdon's soulful vocals and Price's innovative keyboard playing, they first gained notoriety with a recording of "House Of The Rising Sun" ('64), an old black folk song. A string of hits followed, including "It's My Life," "We Gotta Get Out Of This Place," "Don't Bring Me Down," "See See Rider." By 1966 Burdon disbanded the group, which had lost a number of its members. He retained the name as Eric Burdon and the Animals, and recorded such hits as "Monterey," "When I Was Young," "Sky Pilot" and "San Franciscan Nights."

The original Animals have recently regrouped and released an album on I.R.S.

THE ZOMBIES

In 1963, Paul Atkinson, Rodney Argent and Hugh Grundy (the original trio) added Colin Blunstone and Chris Taylor White. They were about to pursue traditional careers when they won a band competition which entitled them to an audition with Decca Records. In 1964-65 the Zombies released two songs with one of the era's most unique sounds, "She's Not There" and "Tell Her No."

THE YARDBIRDS

The Yardbirds are perhaps most remembered for having contained, at one time or another, three of rock's foremost guitar players, Eric Clapton, Jimmy Page and Jeff Beck, whose reign was most successful.

Playing Chicago-style blues, the Yardbirds (Eric Clapton, Keith Relf, Chris Dreja, Paul Sam-

Above: Between 1965 and 1967, Herman's Hermits had many hits.

Below: The Dave Clark Five were actually the first English group to tour America.

well-Smith and Jim McCarty) formed in 1964. They obtained a recording contract early in 1965; and when they replaced the Rolling Stones at the famed Crawdaddy Club in mid-1965 their notoriety increased. Late that year, however, Clapton left and was replaced by Jeff Beck before the Yardbirds had even attained a hit. (Clapton went on to success in landmark groups Cream and Blind Faith, and is presently a solo act.)

1966 brought such hits as "For Your Love," "Shape Of Things To Come" and "Over, Under, Sideways, Down," but in the middle of that year Samwell-Smith departed, replaced by Jimmy Page on bass. When Beck became ill shortly thereafter, Page switched to lead guitar, and with Beck's return both played guitar (Dreja played bass) for the short while that Beck remained. Beck went on to form his own group (including Rod Stewart), and the Yardbirds did not remain together much longer. In October 1968 Page added new members and changed the group's name to Led Zeppelin.

THE KINKS

In 1964 brothers Ray and Dave Davies decided to work full time as musicians. Joining them were Mick Avory and Peter Quaife. As was typical, the group began playing small clubs and were discovered by Shel Talmy, who secured them a recording contract. It was their third single, "You Really Got Me" ('64), that hit, and then "All Day And All Of The Night" ('65). Two more followed with "Tired Of Waiting For You" and "Set Me Free."

Ray Davies' writing became more sophisticated with "Well Respected Man" and "Who'll Be The Next In Line," both of which did well, but the music became somewhat inaccessible for the times and they did not have another hit until 1970 with "Lola." They are still going strong today.

THE SMALL FACES

Next to The Who, the Small Faces were the only other significant mod band. Beginning as the Outcasts, Kenney Jones, Ronnie Lane, Steve Marriott and Ian McLagan became the Small Faces. Although they did not have an abundance of hits ("Itchycoo Park" was their biggest in the U.S. in 1967), they gained a lot of notoriety. In 1969 lead singer Steve Marriott left the group and Jeff Beck band members, first Ron Wood, and then Rod Stewart, joined what then changed to the Faces. The Faces broke up when Ron Wood joined the Rolling Stones, and Rod Stewart, who had had a solo deal throughout, began to become more and more popular.

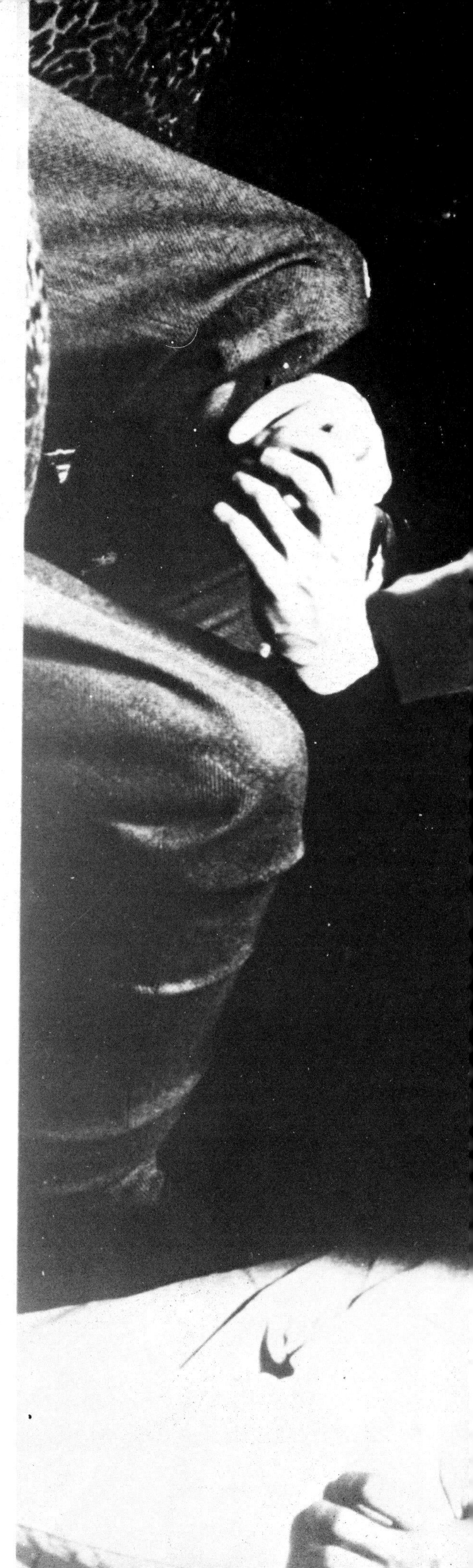

Dave Davies, Ray Davies, John Dalton and Mick Avory were The Kinks, although the original lineup included Peter Quaife. They had their last hit in the mid-'60s, but 1983 brought them back with a hit album, *State of Confusion*.

CHAPTER FIVE

The U.S. Folk, Rock and Pop

Meanwhile, the U.S. was lapping up the English sounds, while undergoing a change by its subtle influence. Groups began to spring up everywhere, yet without the English sound of course, except for the Beau Brummels, a San Francisco band, who had everyone fooled.

In the early '60s folk music was at a peak, with such names as the Chad Mitchell Trio, the Kingston Trio, The Christy Minstrels, and Peter, Paul & Mary. And then everything changed.

BOB DYLAN

Bob Dylan (born Robert Zimmerman) had been playing New York's Greenwich Village coffee houses, and stunning audiences. His influences included blues legend Leadbelly, and some called him the heir to folk legend Woody Guthrie. Dylan was not just a folk artist performing the traditional folk songs of our country as others were; he was a singer-songwriter. It is a contradiction of sorts to say that he was a folk singer, for that implies he was carrying on the legacy of folk material, yet his own material was in that vein for his first few weeks on the scene, and his folk songs spoke to the country's current needs. One of his earliest compositions, "Blowin' In The Wind," was not only recorded by Dylan on his second album, but by the Chad Mitchell Trio, Jerry Jackson, Dennis Rogers, Arthur Lyman, Bob Harter, Jackie DeShannon, Odetta, the Kingston Trio, and Peter, Paul & Mary. It was Peter, Paul & Mary's version that actually hit the top of the charts. Suddenly Dylan was the leader of the protest movement.

In 1962 there had been his debut album, *Bob Dylan,* and in 1963 there was *The Freewheelin' Bob Dylan.* In 1964 *The Times They Are A-Changin'* hit the top of the charts and its title song provided yet another anthem for the war-ridden generation.

By 1964 Dylan had three folk albums to his credit, and in April of that year, or so the story goes, he was driving across Colorado when the sounds of the Beatles on the radio stirred him to change. *Another Side Of Bob Dylan* was a landmark album in 1964, for it contained a number of songs that altered folk: "It Ain't Me Babe," later recorded by the Turtles, "All I Really Want To Do," recorded by the Byrds and Sonny & Cher, "Chimes of Freedom" and "My Back Pages," both recorded by the Byrds.

Although a popular artist, Dylan's first hit was not until 1965 with "Subterranean Homesick Blues," and that was the year the Byrds recorded his "Mr. Tamborine Man" and "All I Really Want To Do" with electric instruments, bringing about the birth of folk rock.

Dylan's folk audience was angered with both his electric hit and his first rock album, *Bringing It All Back Home,* but that never stopped Dylan. That summer he released *Highway 61 Revisited,* which spawned "Like A Rolling Stone," his first major hit, that completely won over rock audiences. That same summer ('65) Dylan further shocked audiences when he had a group, later to become known as the Band, backing him in concert.

In the fall of 1966 *Blonde On Blonde* was recorded with top Nashville session players, something very unusual at that time. The album, issued by Columbia Records, was one of the first nonanthology double albums. In 1968 *John Wesley Harding* took Dylan in yet another style, mixing country with folk rock, and 1969's *Nashville Skyline* expanded that style even more.

1974 returned Dylan to social and political commentaries in *Blood On The Tracks. Desire* was released in 1975, *Street Legal* in 1978 and *Slow Train Coming* in 1979, reflecting his born-again Christian ideals. *Saved* was issued in 1980 and 1981 produced *Shot Of Love.*

THE BYRDS

As mentioned in conjunction with Bob Dylan, the Byrds, even before Dylan, produced the folk-rock sound. It was Dylan's "Mr. Tamborine Man," however, that was the first such sound and the first actual challenge to the English stranglehold on music.

It was 1964 when Roger (born Jim) McGuinn hooked up with David Crosby, Gene Clark, Chris Hillman and Michael Clarke. In 1965 they recorded "Mr. Tamborine Man," which quickly hit Number One on the charts. Interestingly enough, that initial recording only contains one Byrd, McGuinn (Crosby and Clark provided background vocals), for the instrumentation was done by three of the biggest session players: Hal Blaine, Larry Knechtel and Leon Russell. The Byrds' debut album, with the same name as the hit single, contained four Dylan compositions; their second, *Turn! Turn! Turn!*, contained two. The title song, written by Pete Seeger, also reached the top, the second in a long list. "Eight Miles High" ('66) from their third album, *Fifth Dimension,* has the distinction of being one of the first records to be banned for its alleged drug references. "Mr. Spaceman," "So You Want To Be A Rock & Roll Star" and "My Back Pages" are among the group's other hits. Group dissension, however, created many exits and replacements, and never reproduced the sound or success of the original lineup. David Crosby perhaps emerged the most successful in post-Byrd times, with McGuinn, Clark and Hillman later teaming up to record again as the Byrds and under other assorted configurations.

DONOVAN

Those who didn't confuse Donovan with Bob Dylan, usually accused him of being a poor imitation. Actually, the two had very little in common except that they were singular artists and both considered poets. Aside from Donovan's first antiwar protest hit, "Universal Soldier" (actually written by Buffy Sainte-Marie), the poetic styles of the two artists bore very little resemblance. While Dylan wrote political and social commentaries, Donovan wrote more of matters of the heart. Interestingly enough, those album cuts not released as singles were considered far superior to his hits, with the exception perhaps of "Universal Soldier" ('65) and "Catch The Wind" ('65). "Colours" also hit in '65, and a string followed with "Sunshine Superman," "Mellow Yellow," "There Is A Mountain," "Wear Your Love Like Heaven," "Jennifer Juniper," and "Hurdy Gurdy Man."

THE MAMAS AND THE PAPAS

In the spring and summer of 1965 John Phillips and his wife, Michelle, Denny Doherty and Cass Elliot honed their talents in the Virgin Islands before moving to Los Angeles. Producer Lou Adler signed them to Dunhill Records and they began to produce their unique folk-rock sound and a string of hits. Their first album, *If You Can Believe Your Eyes And Ears*, yielded several top songs including "California Dreamin'," "Monday, Monday" and Lennon/McCartney's "I Call Your Name." Their second album, *The Mamas and Papas*, continued their good fortune with "I Saw Her Again" and "Words Of Love," and *Deliver* spawned "Dedicated To The One I Love" and "Creeque Alley." By 1967 the band ended with the death of Mama Cass, as she was called. In recent years, however, John Phillips, his daughter MacKenzie, Denny Doherty and Spanky McFarland (from another '60s band, Spanky and Our Gang) joined forces to revive the Mamas and the Papas.

THE LOVIN' SPOONFUL

In only two years this group managed to create and launch musical classics blending rock, blues, folk and even jug-band, music. They had such hits as "Do You Believe In Magic," "Did You Ever Have To Make Up Your Mind," "You Didn't Have To Be So Nice," "Summer In The City," "Rain On The Roof," "Nashville Cats" and "Darling Be Home Soon." Their career was cut short, however, when Zal Yanovsky, who was busted for drugs and threatened with deportation, turned informant to remain in the country. John Sebastian went on to have moderate success as a solo artist.

THE TURTLES

The Turtles started out in the folk-rock vein with Bob Dylan's "It Ain't Me, Babe" in 1965, but soon altered their style to reflect a pop-whimsical attitude. The original unit of Mark Volman, Howard Kaylan, Al Nichol, Chuck Portz, Jim Turner and Don Murray, altered several times, but Volman and Kaylan remained at the helm. In 1966 they had their second big hit, "You, Baby," and in 1967 they had four hits: "Happy Together," "She'd Rather Be With Me," "You Know What I Mean" and "She's My Girl." In 1968 and 1969 "Eleanor" and "You Showed Me" went high on the charts, and the group disbanded in 1970, although Volman and Kaylan continue to tour as Flo and Eddie.

PAUL REVERE & THE RAIDERS

Paul Revere and the Raiders were one of the first rock groups to sign with Columbia Records in 1963. With the gimmick of Revolutionary War outfits, choreography and their pop-flavored music, they attracted largely a young audience. In 1965 the group came together with Philip Volk and lead singer Mark Lindsay, and they managed their first hit single, "Steppin' Out." "Just Like Me" and "Kicks" followed in '66 and, with the aid of exposure on numerous Dick Clark tours and TV shows, the group, finally known as Paul Revere and the Raiders, starring Mark Lindsay, continued to be a major attraction. In 1969, while still a member of the group, Lindsay decided to attempt a solo career and scored with a top-10 hit, "Arizona." In 1971 the band once again had a hit with "Indian Reservation," but by 1973 both the group and Lindsay had vanished from the charts.

SONNY AND CHER

Because of their hit with Dylan's "All I Really Want To Do," Sonny & Cher are often mistakenly considered a part of the folk-rock scene. Not so. That song, just like all their follow-up hits, was definitely in a pop mold. One of the few successful husband-wife duos in music, Sonny & Cher had their first hit in 1965 with "I Got You, Babe."

Forerunners in the Folk Rock sound, The Byrds (clockwise from bottom right) were Gene Parsons, Clarence White, John York and Roger (also known as Jim) McGuinn.

Paul Revere and the Raiders' Mark Lindsay was lead vocalist and "star" of the group.

Right: The Turtles disbanded in 1970, but not before their five year successful run with several hits. Below Left: The Lovin' Spoonful's Steve Boone, Zal Yanovsky, Joe Butler and John Sebastian. Right: Donovan's first antiwar protest song, "Universal Soldier," was written by Buffy Saint-Marie.

Other hits included "Baby, Don't Go," "The Beat Goes On," "Gypsies, Tramps And Thieves" (Cher) and "Half Breed" (Cher). During mid-1971 they hosted a summer replacement TV show and were signed to do their own show in 1972. They were the first musical act to attract that kind of large TV audience, and *The Sonny and Cher Show* was a winner for a few years.

GARY PUCKETT AND THE UNION GAP

Perhaps the finest vocal prowess of the '60s belonged to Gary Puckett, whose powerfully sung pop ballads gave the group the distinction of having sold more records than anyone else, including the Beatles, in 1968. Clad in Civil War outfits while performing, the band received six consecutive gold records for "Woman, Woman," "Young Girl," "Lady Willpower," "Over You," "Don't Give Into Him" and "This Girl Is A Woman Now." They disbanded in 1971, but their *Greatest Hits* album is still in print and selling steadily.

SIMON AND GARFUNKEL

Probably the most successful duo of the '60s, Paul Simon and Art Garfunkel met as youngsters. In 1957 they recorded "Hey, Schoolgirl" as Tom & Jerry, but their career did not flourish and they went their separate ways. They came back together in 1965 to record their debut album *Wednesday Morning,* but it was their second album, *Sounds Of Silence,* which brought them to the forefront when its title track became a smash. Their sensational harmonies once again were evident on "Homeward Bound," "I Am A Rock," "Dangling Conversation" and "A Hazy Shade Of Winter." "At The Zoo," from *Bookends,* followed, and 1968 brought major success with *The Graduate* soundtrack. As one of the top-grossing films of the decade, *The Graduate* catapulted "Mrs. Robinson" to the top of the charts, winning Simon and Garfunkel the Grammy that year for Best Pop Performance by a Vocal Group. "Bridge Over Troubled Water," their biggest single, was released in 1970 and became a classic. The album of the same name, also containing the hit "Cecilia," was their last as a duo. Garfunkel went on to pursue an acting career in such films as *Catch-22* (1969) and *Carnal Knowledge* (1970) and Paul Simon's solo career began to blossom by 1972. Garfunkel also pursued a successful recording career and the tables turned in 1980 when Simon wrote, scored and starred in *One Trick Pony.* The two reunited in 1981 for a benefit concert in New York's Central Park and some scattered concert appearances worldwide.

THE BUFFALO SPRINGFIELD

Only in existence for a year, the Buffalo Springfield managed to establish itself among the great bands of the '60s. In retrospect, the indelible imprint is understandable, for talent and creativity in that band ran rampant. Nearly all its members have emerged in various other vehicles throughout the past 20 years.

Stephen Stills, Neil Young, Richie Furay, Dewey Martin and Bruce Palmer formed in 1966, were quickly noticed and recorded their first album, which contained the hit "For What It's Worth." "Bluebird" and "Rock And Roll Woman" followed in 1967, with 1968 yielding "Expecting To Fly" and "On The Way Home." Jim Messina produced their third album, played bass, sang and even contributed a tune, but by then the band's inner dissension made it impossible to continue together.

THE YOUNG RASCALS

Felix Cavaliere, Eddie Brigati and Gene Cornish came together in Joey Dee's Starlighters. Cavaliere had met drummer Dino Dannelli on a gig in Las Vegas, and eventually the four formed the Young Rascals, making their debut in New Jersey in 1965. To this day Cavaliere says the musicianship was just average (with the possible exception of Dannelli), but the Cavaliere-Brigati compositions and the sound they created belied that fact. They were the first blue-eyed soul group, the first white band (although for a long time thought to be black) to perform popified R&B and gather a black audience as well as white. In fact, at their concerts, they demanded that a black act be on the bill so the audience would be a guaranteed mixture.

Sid Bernstein, the promoter who brought the Beatles to Shea Stadium, became their manager in 1965. Shortly thereafter they signed with Atlantic Records, and while their first single, "I Ain't Gonna Eat Out My Heart Anymore," only entered the top 50, their second, in 1966, "Good Lovin'," reached Number One. "You Better Run" and "I've Been Lonely Too Long" were also major hits, and on their next album ('67) the title track, "Groovin'," stayed at top position for four weeks and in the top 10 for nine. For the next two years they barraged the charts with several consecutive hits: "A Girl Like You," "How Can I Be Sure," "It's Wonderful," "A Beautiful Morning," "People Got To Be Free" and "A Ray Of Hope." The Rascals (as they had become known) were another one of those bands which ceased because of internal differences and unfortunately terminated prematurely in 1970.

Sounds of Silence brought Simon and Garfunkel well deserved fame, and their soundtrack for *The Graduate* in 1968 made their names household words. By the '70s, they were into solo careers, but 1981 brought them together again for a benefit concert.

The Sonny and Cher of the mid-'60s were part of the hippie generation, but by the early '70s, they were slick and classy on their hit television series, *The Sonny and Cher Show.*

Felix Cavaliere, Eddie Brigati, Gene Cornish and Dino Danelli were The Young Rascals, a group suffering with internal differences throughout its five year run.

CHAPTER SIX

Motown

At the same time, another sound was being developed in Detroit, Michigan. What was to become known as the Motown sound started with one man, Berry Gordy, Jr., and his small independent record label, Tamla. It wasn't too long before several divisions were formed, Motown being the most recognizable.

Motown's beginnings were in the early '60s, and by the mid-'60s, with the legendary songwriting forces Holland-Dozier-Holland behind many of the hits, the popified R&B became one of the most popular sounds and one of the most consistently heard on the radio. Finally soul music had broken through to the pop charts and there it stayed. It is no coincidence that many of the following artists are still with us today. The durability of the music has resulted in the longevity of many of Motown's discoveries.

SMOKEY ROBINSON AND THE MIRACLES

While Berry Gordy gave William "Smokey" Robinson and his group the Miracles their first break, Robinson certainly helped launch Gordy's company. In fact, the Miracles' first hit, "Shop Around," in 1961 was Motown's first claim to fame. Robinson went on to contribute hit compositions for other members of the Motown stable such as Mary Wells, the Temptations and Marvin Gaye. In the mid-'60s, the group had numerous hits, including "Come On, Do The Jerk," "Ooh Baby Baby," "The Tracks Of My Tears," "Going To A Go-Go," "More Love" and "I Second That Emotion." Finally the group became known as Smokey Robinson and the Miracles. Around 1967 Robinson also accepted an executive position at Motown while recording and touring. In 1972, however, he left the group so he could spend more time with his family, and then assumed his role as Motown's vice-president, full time. In 1975 Smokey returned to brief touring and had a hit single in 1979, "Cruisin'." Obviously a testament to his talent, Robinson keeps reemerging and did so again in 1980 with "Being With You."

THE FOUR TOPS

Renaldo Benson, Levi Stubbs, Abdul Fakir and Lawrence Payton had spent nearly a decade honing their craft before any major breakthrough. In 1963 they signed with Motown and "Baby, I Need Your Loving" became one of 1964's big hits. Nonstop Holland-Dozier-Holland compositions kept the Four Tops on top for nearly four years, including such songs as "I Can't Help Myself" ('65), "It's The Same Old Song" ('65), "Something About You" ('65), "Standing in the Shadows of Love" ('66), and "Reach Out I'll Be There" ('66). In 1968, like many of the Motown artists, the Four Tops' success waned with the departure of Holland-Dozier-Holland. They did, however, manage a hit in 1981 with "She Used To Be My Girl."

MARVIN GAYE

Accepting his 1982-83 Grammy award for "Sexual Healing," Gaye said, "I've waited 27 years for this."

Joining up with Gordy and Motown in 1962, Gaye's first single for the company was "Stubborn Kind Of Fellow," followed by Holland-Dozier-Holland's "Can I Get A Witness" (with Mary Wells). In 1964 his big hit was "How Sweet It Is (To Be Loved By You)," and 1965 spawned two of Smokey Robinson's productions, "I'll Be Doggone" and "Ain't That Peculiar." 1966 and '67 included "Take This Heart of Mine" and "Little Darling," and in 1967 he teamed with Tammi Terrell, recording such hits as "Ain't No Mountain High Enough," "Your Precious Love" and "If I Could Build My Whole World Around You." 1968 brought a tremendous hit in "Ain't Nothing But The Real Thing," and later that year "I Heard It Through The Grapevine" gave Gaye perhaps his biggest hit until "Sexual Healing."

THE SUPREMES

Signing with Motown in 1962, the Supremes had their first hit, "Where The Lovelight Starts Shining Through His Eyes," in 1963. Their most significant breakthrough occurred the following year, however, with the first of a string of five hits written by—who else?—Holland-Dozier-Holland. "Where Did Our Love Go" began the phenomenon, followed by "Baby Love," "Come See About Me," "Stop! In The Name Of Love" and "Back In My Arms." 1965's "Nothing But Heartaches" did not achieve the same kind of success, but with the next, "You Can't Hurry Love," another H-D-H string began, including "You Keep Me Hanging On" and "Love Is Here And Now You're Gone."

In 1967 the group began billing itself as Diana Ross and the Supremes and two more H-D-H compositions hit with "Reflections" and "In And Out Of Love." "Love Child" followed in 1968 and "Someday We'll Be Together " in 1969. At that time the Supremes paired up with the Temptations for an album and hit with "I'm Gonna Make You Love Me," but by the end of '69 Ross left the group to work as a solo artist. The biggest hit the Supremes had after Ross departed was a teaming with the Four Tops on "River Deep, Mountain High."

Ross, on the other hand, continued to do remarkably well with "Reach Out And Touch (Somebody's Hand)" and "Ain't No Mountain High Enough," and although her recording career began to wane, she has never been far from the public eye. In 1972 she starred in *Lady Sings The Blues*, in which she played the legendary Billie Holiday, and in 1975 she starred in *Mahogany* and hit the charts with the film's theme song, "Do You Know Where You're Going To?" In 1978 she starred in *The Wiz*, an all-black version of *The Wizard Of Oz*, and in the '80s once more enjoyed the success of "I'm Coming Out," "It's My Turn," "Endless Love" (duet with Lionel Richie), "Why Do Fools Fall In Love" and "Muscles," written and produced by Michael Jackson.

THE TEMPTATIONS

Perhaps the male version of the Supremes, the Temptations accumulated an abundance of commercial hits for Motown. Smokey Robinson co-wrote and produced their first 1964 hit, "The Way You Do The Things You Do," and the classic "My Girl." Other hits during that time were "It's Growing," "Since I Lost My Baby," "My Baby" and "Get Ready." Through 1968, Norman Whitfield co-wrote and produced such hits as "Ain't Too Proud To Beg," "Beauty Is Only Skin Deep," "(I Know) I'm Losing You" and "I Wish It Would Rain." In 1970 the Temptations hit with the classic "I Can't Get Next To You," and in 1972 they scored again with "Papa Was A Rollin' Stone." The band continued through the '70s despite various personnel changes, but never reached the heights of the '60s.

Left: Diana Ross has been a hit maker for over 20 years, on records and film. Her 1983 *Muscles* LP, was produced by Michael Jackson, whose career she helped start in the late '60s. Below: The Temptations' first hit was co-written by Smokey Robinson.

CHAPTER SEVEN San Francisco and The

Jimi Hendrix, known as rock music's first black superstar, laid the groundwork for the coming heavy metal groups.

The most popular British "psychedlic" group, Cream's Eric Clapton, Jack Bruce and Ginger Baker got together in 1966. Eric later went on to perform as a solo act.

Psychedelic Sound

While Motown was going strong in Detroit, San Francisco was giving birth to a new sound. Art is always a reflection of a time's sociological factors, and the new music was no exception. It was a time when young people became discouraged with adult society, were fed up with war, dropped out of society and dropped acid (LSD). They became known as "hippies," spawning antiwar demonstrations, pleas for flower power (peace), love-ins, and questioning societal morals with a new awareness fired by the so-called expansion of the mind by hallucinogens, which were the crutch of the times. Psychedelic music mirrored all of it.

THE JEFFERSON AIRPLANE

In 1966 the Jefferson Airplane was the first San Francisco group to obtain a major recording contract, and thereby the first recognized "psychedelic" band. By the time of their debut album, *Jefferson Airplane Takes Off* (Sept. '66), their lead vocalist, Signe Tile Anderson, had departed to have a baby and was replaced by Grace Slick. It was their second album, *Surrealistic Pillow,* that actually launched their career when "Somebody To Love" hit high on the charts and was followed by one of the first blatantly drug-oriented songs, "White Rabbit." While they did not have another major hit, their albums such as *After Bathing At Baxters* ('68), *Crown of Creation* ('68), *Bless Its Pointed Little Head* ('69) and *Volunteers* ('69), sold extremely well. Their live performances, too, attracted attention with the first usage of psychedelic light shows.

The unit began to crack, however, with Marty Balin's exit in 1971 and the band's subsequent releases did not do so well. Various solo attempts and projects added to the chaos, and by 1974 the group had faded. A new band, however, called the Jefferson Starship, rose from the dust and included, at first, two key members of the Airplane, Slick and Paul Kantner. For their first album ('74), the third integral member, Marty Balin, returned. The time for psychedelic music had passed, and by 1975 and their first hit, "Miracles," a whole new generation was listening to their now pop-oriented music.

THE GRATEFUL DEAD

The Grateful Dead, to this day, has maintained an uncommercial attitude towards music, and though they never celebrated a hit single they remain one of the institutions from that time. From their first Warner Bros. release, *The Grateful Dead,* the band has gathered a strong and loyal following. Their live concerts were considered events and their 1970 nonstudio album, *Live Dead,* captured some of that energy. From 1974-1977 the band was not active, but 1977's *The Grateful Dead Movie* revived their popularity. Signing with Arista (after their own record company failed), they have been recording ever since.

COUNTRY JOE AND THE FISH

Another band with little radio exposure, but one that emerged in grand style from San Francisco, was Country Joe and the Fish. Psychedelic-jug-band music was its forte, and humor and politics created such commentaries as "I Feel Like I'm Fixin' To Die Rag" and "A Vietnam Veteran's Still Alive."

BIG BROTHER AND THE HOLDING COMPANY (AND JANIS JOPLIN)

After their appearance at the famed Monterey Pop Festival where Bob Dylan's manager signed them, the band's lead singer, Janis Joplin, became the Queen of Acid Rock.

Following the Jefferson Airplane's lead of a female focal point, Joplin was added to the Holding Company and immediately gained them national prominence. Her gutsy, raw vocals and her soulful deliveries brought a new feminine sexuality to music. She only recorded two albums with the band, *Big Brother And The Holding Company* ('67), which yielded the hit "Piece Of My Heart," and *Cheap Thrills* ('68), after which she left to pursue a solo career. The band folded shortly thereafter and Joplin only stayed alive long enough to record two solo albums. *I Got Dem Ol' Kozmic Blues Again Mama,* released in 1969, contained the hit "Try," and she was found dead in her apartment on October 4, 1970, a victim of her heroin habit. *Pearl* was released posthumously, featuring her classic performance of Kris Kristofferson's "Me And Bobby McGee."

SANTANA

At the time known for its unique blending of Latin music and psychedelia, Santana began in 1967. Signed with Columbia Records, their premiere album, *Santana,* spawned two hit singles, "Jingo" ('69) and "Evil Ways" ('70). In 1970 their second album also brought forth two hits, "Black Magic Woman" and "Oye Como Va." By 1973 Carlos Santana was the only remaining original member; growing with the times and away from the psychedelic sound, several jazz-oriented records followed. Currently in the '80s, he is still going strong with pop-flavored offerings.

JIMI HENDRIX

Although its leader was American born, the Jimi Hendrix Experience was one of the few English imports to create a wave in psychedelia (perhaps Cream is the only other band with that distinction). Hendrix, rock music's first black superstar, is revered to be one of the greatest guitarists of our times. Experimental and innovative, his group's debut album, *Are You Experienced?*, was high on British charts when they took the U.S. by storm at 1967's Monterey Pop Festival. That album included such classics as "Purple Haze," "Hey Joe" and "Foxy Lady." Their second album, *Axis: Bold As Love*, was another big seller, but their third and final release, *Electric Ladyland* ('68), spawned their only big hit, Bob Dylan's "All Along The Watchtower."

In 1969 the band announced their break-up and Hendrix spent most of his time out of the public eye. At the height of his career, Hendrix died of a drug overdose on September 18, 1970. He will long be remembered for his unique style and daring showmanship, laying the groundwork for the coming heavy metal groups and influencing guitarists everywhere.

CREAM

Probably the most popular British "psychedelic" group was Cream. The trio was comprised of Eric Clapton, Jack Bruce and Ginger Baker, and, along with Jimi Hendrix, paved the way for countless "power trios" throughout rock music.

Sparked by the R&B movement initiated by Alexis Korner and Cyril Davies in England, the three got together in 1966 and obtained a recording contract almost immediately. Although the group's lifespan was short, their albums, most notably *Fresh Cream, Disraeli Gears* and *Wheels Of Fire,* became classics.

THE DOORS

One of the biggest and most commercially successful bands of the psychedelic era was another non-San Francisco group, The Doors.

Jim Morrison and Ray Manzarek met while both were attending classes at the University of California, Los Angeles. When it came time to form a group, organist Ray contacted drummer John Densmore, whom he had previously met, and John subsequently brought guitarist Robbie Krieger into the fold. Finally getting a gig at Hollywood's Whisky A Go-Go as the house band, they were spotted by Jac Holzman of Elektra Records and immediately signed. Their first album, *The Doors,* was a smash, and by mid-'67, "Light My Fire" (one of rock's first extended pieces, lasting seven minutes) reached the top of the charts. (The album also contained the 11-minute "The End.") Their next album, *Strange Days,* spawned two hits, "People Are Strange" and "Love Me Two Times." By their third album, *Waiting For The Sun,* in 1968, however, Morrison had begun getting drunk and/or stoned most of the time. It was a difficult album in the making, but did yield a hit, "Hello, I Love You." *The Soft Parade,* the following year, also sported a hit, "Touch Me," but 1970's *Morrison Hotel* did not offer even one hit.

By now Morrison had become a major celebrity. One of rock's most charismatic figures, however, he became shrouded in controversy when busted in Miami for "indecent exposure" (Ray Manzarek still disputes the charge). His erratic personality had made it difficult to record and perform live, but *L.A. Woman,* their 1971 offering, returned the heart to their music. Sans producer Paul Rothschild, the Doors concentrated on recapturing their original spark and spontaneity and came up with two hits, "Love Her Madly" and "Riders On The Storm."

On July 3, 1971, while in Paris for rest and relaxation, Jim Morrison died. The other three persisted with two more albums, *Other Voices* and *Full Circle,* but the thread that had unified them was gone. Even though Krieger had written their hits, it was Morrison's poetic magic that was the core of their musical unity.

In 1978 the remaining Doors completed a project Morrison had begun while he was still alive. *An American Prayer* is an album of Morrison's recorded poetry with musical backing, the Doors' final tribute to Jim Morrison. In 1983 they also released a live album.

Above: (From Left), Santana's Armando Peraza, Carlos Santana, Greg Walker, Leon Chancler, David Brown and Tom Coster.

Below: (From Left), Jim Morrison, John Densmore, Robby Krieger and Ray Manzarek (bottom) were the Doors.

The Nitty Gritty Dirt Band first scored in 1967 and were later among the first bands to feature a 1950s nostalgia routine in their act. Although the lineup changed a bit they were the first American band to tour Russia in 1977.

CHAPTER EIGHT

Country-Rock

Toward the latter part of the '60s, in contrast to the psychedelic scene, folk rock was still developing and had taken on a maturation and sophistication as exemplified by Simon and Garfunkel. Prior to this, in the early '60s, California music had been represented by surf boards and race cars, a style embodied by the Beach Boys. But, finally, various elements of rock began to be combined to create new sounds, typical of what became known as the "L.A. sound." Carried well into the '70s and '80s, many artists of this sound are still around today.

NITTY GRITTY DIRT BAND

Few people realize the instrumental role this band had in the formation of L.A.'s country-rock scene. Always one (or 10 as the case may be) step ahead of everyone else, they rarely reap the benefits of recognition. For example, in the late '60s this band was playing country-swing, a decade before the Urban Cowboy country-swing craze occurred. They were also among the first bands to feature a '50s nostalgia routine in their act, which was later made famous by such groups as Sha Na Na. More important, however, was that the Nitty Gritty Dirt Band was a forerunner in mixing country and rock. They were among the first groups to become known for their instrumental virtuosity and to feature material by up-and-coming local songwriters like Jackson Browne, Randy Newman, Michael Nesmith and Kenny Loggins.

First scoring in 1967 with "Buy For Me The Rain," a mild melodic folk song, the Dirt Band remained popular but didn't have another big hit until 1971, with "Mr. Bojangles." Perhaps one of their most notable contributions was an album called *Will The Circle Be Unbroken,* recorded in 1972 in Nashville with such country legends as Maybelle Carter, Roy Acuff and Earl Scruggs.

In 1977 they were America's first band to tour Russia. Chosen over many groups who had certainly racked up more hits than the Dirt Band, they were picked as the best example for incorporating traditional American folk with rock. It wasn't until 1979 that they had another hit with "An American Dream" and 1980 with "Make A Little Magic." Still containing three founding members, Jeff Hanna, John McEuen, and Jimmie Fadden, plus Jimmy Ibbotson who joined in 1969, they are still going strong and 1983 saw a country hit with "Shot Full of Love."

POCO

In 1968, at L.A.'s prime music club, the Troubadour, the Nitty Gritty Dirt Band headlined with a band called Poco (actually first called Pogo) opening the show. Formed by two ex-Buffalo Springfield members, Richie Furay and Jim Messina, Poco expanded its original folk-rock roots to include elements of country. (At one time or another, Randy Meisner and Timothy B. Schmit were also in the band.) Although the band (now including only one original member, Rusty Young) has been recording through the years and has gathered a loyal audience, they did not score with a big hit until 1979's "Crazy Love" and "Heart Of The Night."

CROSBY, STILLS & NASH (& YOUNG)

In the meanwhile, another Buffalo Springfield member, Stephen Stills, joined ex-Byrds' David Crosby and ex-Hollies' Graham Nash to form Crosby, Stills & Nash. Known for their magnificent harmonies, their first album in 1969 yielded two hits, "Marrakesh Express" and "Suite: Judy Blue Eyes." That same year Neil Young (also an ex-Buffalo Springfield member) joined the band and they recorded another classic album, *Deja Vu,* featuring Joni Mitchell's "Woodstock," "Teach Your Children" and "Our House." Throughout the years members have pursued solo careers (most successfully, Neil Young) and worked with one another in various configurations, always concert draws and still recording hits.

LOGGINS AND MESSINA

When Jim Messina left Poco in 1971, his intention was to produce acts instead of performing with them. That year Messina was set to produce a new singer-songwriter by the name of Kenny Loggins, whose only real accomplishment was having the Nitty Gritty Dirt Band record four of his songs on their *Uncle Charlie* album. Messina's input was so expansive, however, the album ended up being called *Kenny Loggins With Jim Messina Sittin' In.* Naturally, Columbia Records would not stand for a hit album from a duo, half of which would not tour, so Messina was persuaded to do so. Seven albums produced many major hits such as "Danny's Song," "Holiday Hotel," "Watchin' The River Run," "Listen To A Country Song" and "Your Mama Don't Dance."

In 1977 the team split to pursue independent careers, and while thus far Messina's has been fairly unsuccessful, Loggins has become a consistently popular major act. By 1983 he had recorded four platinum-plus albums, each spawning one or more hits.

LINDA RONSTADT

Linda Ronstadt is perhaps the top female vocalist of the last decade. She did not attain stardom until 1975, but her notable beginnings were in the late '60s, her music of the "L.A. sound."

In 1964 she moved from her birthplace, Tucson, Arizona, to Los Angeles, where she and guitarist friend Bobby Kimmel were joined by Kenny Edwards to form the Stone Poneys. Capitol Records released her first album in 1967, which gained little attention. Her second and last album with Kimmel and Edwards, *Evergreen—Volume 2,* gave Linda her only big hit through those years, "Different Drum" by Mike Nesmith of the Monkees.

Left And Below: Linda Ronstadt was considered a country pop artist until 1975 when she released her *Heart Like A Wheel* album and gained recognition across the board. Through the '70s and into the '80s she incorporated more rock into her music and successfully tested the waters of Broadway stage and film.

Kenny Loggins and Jim Messina were a hit making duo from 1971 until their split in 1977. Kenny went on to be a platinum album seller and continues to produce hits today.

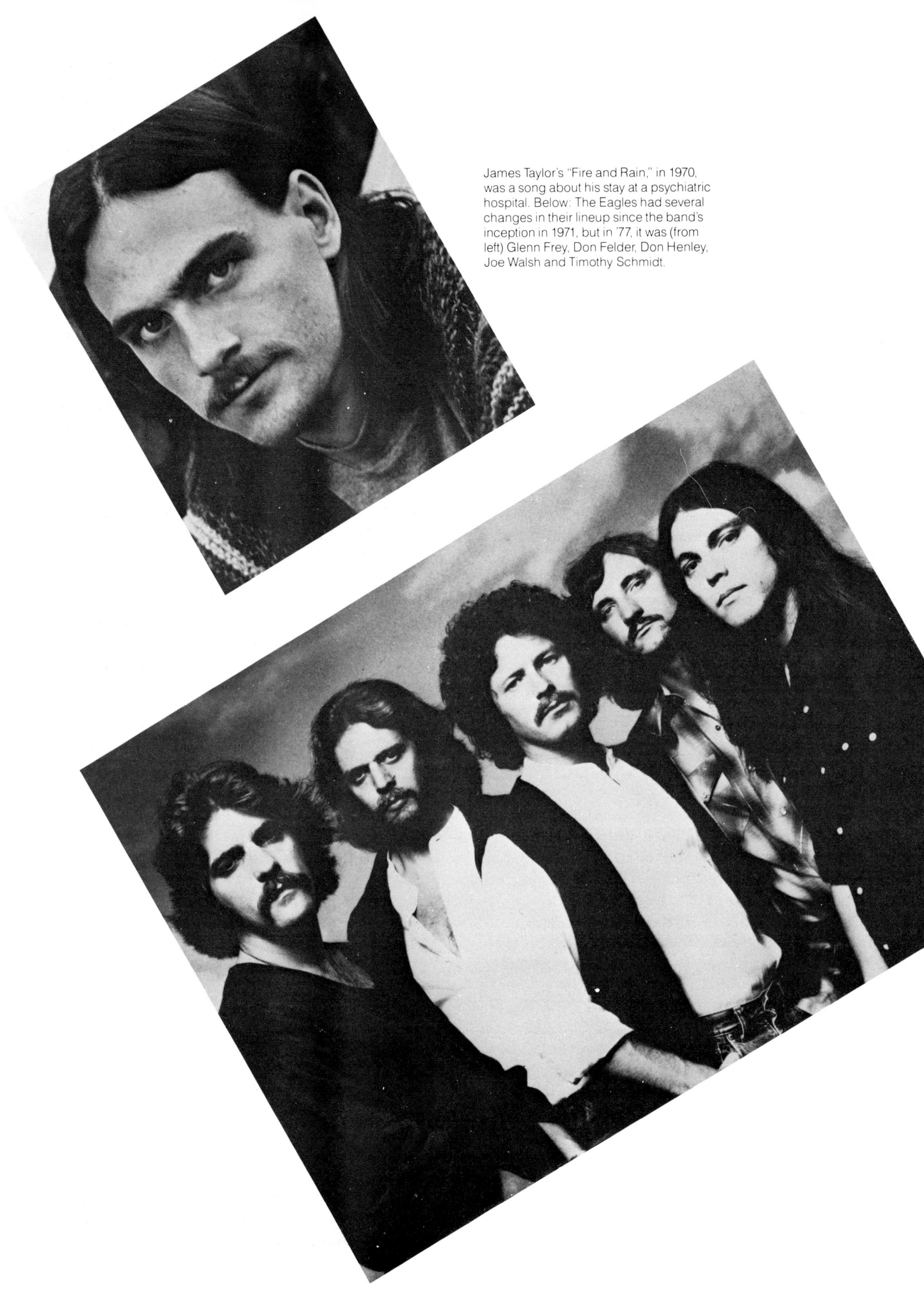

James Taylor's "Fire and Rain," in 1970, was a song about his stay at a psychiatric hospital. Below: The Eagles had several changes in their lineup since the band's inception in 1971, but in '77, it was (from left) Glenn Frey, Don Felder, Don Henley, Joe Walsh and Timothy Schmidt.

Not a songwriter but rather an interpreter, she utilized the talents of such up-and-coming songwriters as Nesmith, J. D. Souther, Randy Newman and Jackson Browne. In 1970 she had another big hit with "Long, Long Time," and two years later a minor hit with Browne's "Rock Me On The Water." In 1971 her back-up group included such future Eagles as Glenn Frey, Don Henley, Bernie Leadon and Randy Meisner.

Too often, however, Ronstadt was dismissed as a country artist until 1975. Meeting up with producer Peter Asher (from Peter and Gordon) became her major breakthrough when he produced her last Capitol album, *Heart Like A Wheel.* Asher became her manager, negotiated a deal with Elektra/Asylum Records, and has since produced all her albums, each seemingly a bigger success than the last. After *Simple Dreams* she began to incorporate even more pop and rock into her albums, recording such hits as Chuck Berry's "Back In The U.S.A.," Smokey Robinson's "Ooh, Baby, Baby" and "Just One Look." *Mad Love* took her further into rock and roll with the inclusion of three Elvis Costello songs and a remake of a Little Anthony and the Imperials' hit, "Hurts So Bad." 1982's *Get Closer* produced another smash success for Ronstadt with its title track and "Easy for You To Say," released after her role in Broadway's *Pirates Of Penzance.* She also played the lead in the film version.

JACKSON BROWNE

As indicated by those who recorded his material early on, Jackson Browne was a singer-songwriter who embodied the L.A. sound.

He started as a member of the original lineup of the Nitty Gritty Dirt Band for a brief time, and although his songs were consistently recorded by other artists, Browne did not really achieve any notoriety in his own right until the '70s. In 1971 he had his first success with "Doctor My Eyes," from his debut album, also containing "Jamaica Say You Will" and "Rock Me On The Water." In 1972, after touring with Joni Mitchell, Browne's "Take It Easy" (co-written by Glenn Frey) launched the Eagles' career. It was not until 1976 that Browne was recognized as a major talent with the release of his *The Pretender* album and the hit "Here Come Those Tears Again." *Running On Empty* entirely established his career with both the title song and a remake of 1961's "Stay" and all his subsequent offerings have been anticipated and acclaimed by fans and critics alike.

JAMES TAYLOR

Peter Asher produced *James Taylor* in 1968 on the Beatles' Apple Record label, but it was not until 1970 that *Sweet Baby James* was released on the Warner Bros. label, a deal Asher had obtained for the musician. "Fire And Rain," a song about Taylor's stay at McLean Psychiatric Hospital in Belmont, Massachusetts, became a huge success.

In 1971 *Mud Slide Slim* was released and Taylor had a hit with Carole King's "You've Got A Friend," and a moderate hit with "Long Ago And Far Away." 1972's *One-Man Dog* included Carole King, Linda Ronstadt and Taylor's then wife, Carly Simon, on vocals and contained a major hit, "Don't Let Me Be Lonely Tonight." His 1975 album *Gorilla* included the hit "How Sweet It Is (To Be Loved By You)," a hit for Marvin Gaye in the '60s, written by Holland-Dozier-Holland. His last Warner Bros. album, *In The Pocket,* yielded "Shower The People," and, after switching to Columbia, his debut *JT* was a huge success that included the hit remake of "Handy Man" (originally a hit for Jimmy Jones in 1960) as well as "Your Smiling Face." 1979's *Flag* offered the hit "Up On The Roof," and Taylor is still going strong.

THE EAGLES

A continuation of the L.A. country-rock sound, the Eagles took us into the '70s. By and far the most popular band of its genre, the group was formed in 1971 by Bernie Leadon, Glenn Frey, Don Henley and Randy Meisner. They had a smash hit with "Take It Easy," a Glenn Frey-Jackson Browne composition, on their debut album, while "Witchy Woman" and "Peaceful, Easy Feeling," were also hits.

Shortly after their second, less successful, album, *Desperado,* Don Felder joined for their third offering, *On The Border,* containing a couple of moderate hits and their chart topper, "Best Of My Love." 1975's *One Of These Nights* had three huge hits: "Lyin' Eyes," "Take It To The Limit" and the title track. Bernie Leadon left the group and was replaced with Joe Walsh, bringing in their breakthrough album, *Hotel California,* in 1976. "New Kid In Town," "Life In The Fast Lane" and the title track all became big hits, the latter two marking a rougher rock edge than their previous mellower country-rock offerings.

In 1977 Randy Meisner departed, replaced with ex-Poco member Timothy B. Schmit, and finally in 1979, *The Long Run* made it to the top of the LP charts with "Heartache Tonight," "I Can't Tell You Why" and the title cut proving winners as singles. It was to be their final album, for the group gave their farewell tour in 1980. Since then, however, all members throughout the run of the Eagles have offered solo projects.

FLEETWOOD MAC

CHAPTER NINE

In 1967 Fleetwood Mac was not even close to the band we know today, in personnel or music. They had just formed that year, with Peter Green, Mick Fleetwood and John McVie all having worked in John Mayall's Bluesbreakers for varying times. Peter and Mick had met in 1966 while working in organist Peter Barden's group, Peter B's Looners. That group evolved into Shotgun Express (with the addition of vocalists Rod Stewart and Beryl Marsden), and Green left two months later to join John Mayall. Fleetwood continued with the group until the unit ceased to be, and in April of 1967 was asked to take over the drum seat in Mayall's band, then was requested to leave after a month. Just two months later Green left Mayall to begin his own group, and recruited Fleetwood. McVie, who had been with Mayall for four years, took some persuading, but finally consented to join the group, dubbed Peter Green's Fleetwood Mac. Jeremy Spencer, record producer Mike Vernon's discovery, was asked to join, and the band proceeded to record its debut album. *Peter Green's Fleetwood Mac*, released in early '68 on Blue Horizon Records, was true to the band's blues background: authentic and devoid of any pop or rock elements. The album stayed on the British charts for 13 months, 17 weeks of which it was in the top 10, achieving for them instant Beatle-like success. When the album was released in the U.S. later that year, the group did their first tour of the States.

Before recording their second album, *Mr. Wonderful*, that same year, a third guitarist, Danny Kirwan, was added to the front lineup. They embarked on a second U.S. tour and recorded a third album, which included such rock standards as "Albatross," "One Sunny Day" and "Black Magic Woman."

Then Play On followed in 1969, marking their debut on Reprise/Warner Records, but in 1970 Peter Green suddenly left the group, causing them to cancel a tour. The group released *Kiln House* with additional vocals by Christine Perfect (also a classically trained pianist) later that year.

The following year, while in Los Angeles, Jeremy Spencer simply didn't show up for their first night of a four-night run at the Whisky A Go-Go. Clifford Davis, their manager, contacted the police and five days later found Spencer at the Children of God Colony, a religious sect, where he chose to remain. Peter Green, however, lent a helping hand by joining the band on the road until the tour's completion. Finally they found a replacement for Spencer, American guitarist/vocalist Bob Welch, and their fifth album, *Future Games*, was released, with Welch writing the title track. That same summer Blue Horizon Records released *Fleetwood Mac In Chicago*, an album recorded in early '69 at Chess Records with several blues legends, including Walter "Shakey" Horton, Willie Dixon and Otis Spann.

In 1972 *Bare Trees* was released, on which Kirwan, Welch and Christine Perfect McVie (now John's wife) handled all the songwriting and vocals. Included on this album was a tune penned by Welch called "Sentimental Lady" (later re-recorded by Welch to launch his solo career).

Since Kirwan had exited in 1972, their next album, *Penguin* (which became their logo), was released in 1973 featuring guitarist Bob Weston (late of Long John Baldry's band) and singer Dave Walker (late of Savoy Brown), who was only a member for this album.

In the fall of 1973, however, while preparing to tour behind the new release *Mystery To Me*, Mick Fleetwood discovered that his wife, Jenny, and his guitarist, Weston, were having an affair. Needless to say, Weston was fired and the band broke up briefly. (Manager Clifford Davis put together a group of other musicians, calling them the New Fleetwood Mac so he wouldn't have to cancel the tour. The genuine Fleetwood Mac filed suit against Davis and, of course, won.)

Mick Fleetwood picked up the pieces of his personal and musical life. He got back together with his wife (they later divorced), reformed the band, and became its manager until 1979, when the band members decided to manage themselves cooperatively as a unit.

"I tend to bind things together, and if something is falling apart I seem to be the one who gets off his ass and does something about it," Fleetwood explains.

In 1974 *Heroes Are Hard To Find* was released, and with the change of management the band changed its locale to Los Angeles, where fate would have Mick stumble across Stevie Nicks and Lindsay Buckingham.

In the late '60s Stevie (Stephanie) Nicks found herself invited into a San Francisco group, Fritz, in which Lindsay Buckingham played bass. (He had originally played guitar, but Fritz had changed him to bass.) Since the band was strictly business, it wasn't until it disbanded in 1971 that Stevie and Lindsay pursued a romantic relationship as well as a musical combination. Just as they were planning to move to Los Angeles, Lindsay contracted mononucleosis and, while they had to postpone their move, he had the time to hone his talents on guitar. Upon their arrival in Los Angeles, through their friend Keith Olsen they were able to land a record deal with Anthem Records, a company which folded even before recording the first project. One of Anthem's owners, however, took the duo with him when he went to Polydor Records. Nicks and Buckingham made their first album, *Buckingham Nicks*, but Polydor refused the second-album option and, once again, the two were without a label.

Lindsay was doing odd jobs and touring in Don Everley's back-up band and Stevie was waiting tables for $1.50 an hour when Mick Fleetwood inadvertently came across them. He was searching for a studio in which to record their next album and happened into Sound City, where engineer Keith Olsen played him one of the *Buckingham Nicks* album cuts to display the studio's facilities. Stevie and Lindsay happened to be next door making a demo when they heard one of their tunes blasting through the studio and went to investigate. Introductions were made, and when Bob Welch suddenly quit at Christmastime, Fleetwood had Keith Olsen inform Stevie and Lindsay that they were his first choice for replacement. Without an audition, they accepted and immediately set about cutting what would be a landmark album, *Fleetwood Mac*. Most of the tunes had previously and independently been written, such as "Chrystal," which was actually on the duo's only album, and "Monday Morning," "Landslide," and "Rhiannon," which had already been demoed for their aborted second release.

Christine McVie's "Over My Head" gave Fleetwood Mac its first American hit and the band proceeded on a lengthy tour. Another hit followed in "Rhiannon" and then "Say You Love Me," and a year after its initial release *Fleetwood Mac* went to Number One on the national charts for the first time. That magical combination that bands seek and hope for had arrived. The songwriting provided a new accessibility in a pop-rock format, and on stage Stevie Nicks provided an identity which had never before been available to the group.

"It's just chemistry," Fleetwood states in an effort to explain the major success that hit the group. "A lot of people ask me, 'Did you know that this was going to happen when Stevie and Lindsay joined the group?' Of course not, but we just knew we liked each other and enjoyed each other's music outside of being involved as a band, and that was it. It's like asking someone why a relationship fell apart. It just did. You can go on talking about it forever, but the end result is that you don't get on. Musically, it's the same thing. That's why people play together and the longer they're together means the longer they can identify and grow without having problems."

That, however, is an extremely optimistic attitude on Fleetwood's part, for ever since their follow-up album, *Rumours*, rumors have consistently circulated as to the status of the group. Knowledge of internal problems and struggles have been made public by the press, and although the band has indeed stayed together, its unity always seems tenuous.

It wasn't until a year and a half after the *Fleetwood Mac* album that *Rumours* was completed and released. Actually, the problems began prior to *Rumours* when John and Christine separated halfway through the initial tour with Lindsay and Stevie. At about the same time Lindsay and Stevie split, and by the time they were to go into the studio to record, neither couple was speaking to one another and Mick Fleetwood was in the middle of his divorce. Somehow, however, the rampant unhappiness seemed to create a bond and mutual compassion, which spurred *Rumours*. In addition to the personal problems, it was a difficult album technically, since the first studio they recorded at for nine weeks in Northern California had a recording machine which destroyed much of their efforts. They journeyed to Miami's

hristine McVie

Stevie Nicks

Mick Fleetwood

John McVie

Lindsey Buckingham

Criteria Studios next, but the album predominately ended up being recorded in Hollywood.

The album spawned several major hits such as "Dreams" (Nicks), "Don't Stop" (McVie), "Go Your Own Way" (Buckingham), and "You Make Loving Fun" (McVie), winning the Grammy for best album of the year and selling over 16 milion copies.

Now, however, the time spent in the studio was becoming even more excessive. This time without those inconveniencing technical mishaps, Fleetwood Mac didn't deliver their next album, *Tusk,* for two years. Explaining their recording techniques and philosophies, Fleetwood Mac offers, "We produce ourselves in the studio and we grow a lot as a band in the studio. We try not to repeat ourselves, yet when you're faced with the same five people, which, of course, we're happy about, you have to try to keep it fresh. The time spent is not because we just sit around, although, of course, that does happen sometimes, but primarily we work all the time. We choose to do that and it's really as simple as that. We are perfectly capable of *not* spending that amount of time, but we're learning more and more in the studio. Perhaps we're learning how to become *less* technical in the studio, using very sophisticated machinery in the proper way without letting it use you. That's a real danger. We also write a lot and reconstruct a lot of stuff in the studio and we scrap things and redo them. We're perfectionists to the point where it may be worth it to scrap something because it's gotten too perfect and try to get it until there's a good feel. If we're going to spend a lot of time on something, we're very aware of not getting it so together that it doesn't feel anything anymore. Plus, nothing gets done unless everyone thinks it's a good idea, so that can be time consuming as well. Luckily, we all think and feel pretty much the same, and though it's not as quick as having someone standing there with a whip telling you what to do, it's the magic of this band."

Tusk, a double album, received mixed reviews. Some hailed it as ambitious and innovative and others criticized it as self-indulgent. Regardless, it spawned two hits, "Sara" and "Think About Me," and did become a quadruple platinum seller.

It was actually almost a three-year period before the next Fleetwood Mac album was released (aside from the live album in 1980), but with good reason. 1981 saw the release of three solo albums, Fleetwood's *The Visitor,* recorded in Ghana, Nicks' *Bella Donna* and Buckingham's *Law And Order.* Both Nicks' and Buckingham's projects did extremely well, and additional solo projects are expected from all, including Christine.

After all the solo projects, the public and critics alike were surprised that Fleetwood Mac remained an entity at all. In June 1982, however, *Mirage* was released with two single hits, "Gypsy" and "Hold Me," but it is impossible to predict the future of the band. With five consecutive albums (including the live album), it marks the first such feat for the group with the same personnel. But considering the resiliency of Mick Fleetwood, if the band ended tomorrow it would not be surprising if there were yet another Fleetwood Mac in the coming.

Ever since Fleetwood Mac's *Rumours* LP, rumors have circulated about the group's unity. In 1981 three members released solo albums, but the following year another group project, *Mirage*, was released. It was their fifth consecutive album with the same group members.

Above: Joni Mitchell's beginnings were in folk rock, but she always was open to experimenting, blending and changing.

Below: Chicago came on the scene at th end of the '60s and are still delivering hit in the '80s.

CHAPTER TEN

THE SEVENTIES

BLOOD, SWEAT AND TEARS

he '60s ended with still another kind of new sound, the fusion of rock and jazz, best exemplified by Blood, Sweat and Tears and Chicago.

Blood, Sweat and Tears was the first group to fully utilize horns as a part of their sound. In New York, in 1967, Al Kooper, Steve Katz and Bobby Colomby began to form BS&T. Soon Fred Lipsius, Randy Brecker, Jerry Weiss and Dick Halligan were added to the group. Signed to Columbia Records, their first album, *Child Is Father To The Man* ('68), was a popular-selling album, even though it had no hits. Founder Al Kooper left shortly after its release and lead vocalist David Clayton-Thomas was added. The second album, *Blood, Sweat & Tears*, more than made up for the earlier with "And When I Die," "God Bless The Child," "Spinning Wheel" and "You've Made Me So Very Happy." Their third album yielded "Hi-De-Ho" and "Lucretia MacEvil." By 1973, however, the group had undergone mass personnel changes and never had a major hit again.

CHICAGO

More rock-oriented, durable and long-lasting than BS&T was a group formed in Chicago. With a career that still continues today, 1982 saw Chicago's 16th album and a Number One hit single, "Hard To Say I'm Sorry." Some of their classic hits include "Does Anybody Really Know What Time It Is," "Make Me Smile," "25 Or 6 To 4," "Just You 'n' Me," "Saturday In The Park," "Happy Man," "Feeling Stronger Every Day," "Beginnings," "If You Leave Me Now," "Baby, What A Big Surprise." As long as the group continues, there will no doubt be many more to add to the list.

JONI MITCHELL

Joni Mitchell has been one of the most highly acclaimed women in music since the latter '60s. While her beginnings were in folk rock, Mitchell is still blending styles, experimenting and changing.

She was signed to Reprise Records in 1967 while Tom Rush recorded her "Circle Game" and "Urge For Going" on a 1968 release, and Judy Collins' hit of Mitchell's "Both Sides Now" brought Mitchell her first taste of notoriety. Mitchell's debut album, *Joni Mitchell* or *Song To A Seagull*, as it was known, produced by David Crosby, went fairly unnoticed. Her second, *Clouds*, gained her more prominence with the single "Chelsea Morning" and her own version of "Both Sides Now." *Ladies Of The Canyon* became a bestseller and her first gold record, and her "Woodstock" (also recorded by Crosby, Stills, Nash & Young) became one of the generation's anthems. *Blue* was her last album for Reprise before moving to Asylum Records where she recorded *For The Roses* and scored with "You Turn Me On, I'm A Radio." Her jazz influences were becoming more noticeable, and finally, on *Court And Spark*, those changes were fully realized with the addition of Tom Scott and the L.A. Express. "Help Me" and "Free Man In Paris" were hits from that album, which became one of the period's most popular. She toured with Tom Scott and the L.A. Express in 1974 and *Miles Of Aisles*, a live double-record produced another major hit, "Big Yellow Taxi." *Hissing Of Summer Lawns* ('75) and *Hejira* followed, utilizing such jazz musicians as Jaco Pastorius and Larry Carlton. Pastorius and Weather Report co-member Wayne Shorter, as well as Latin percussionist Airto, were key figures on Mitchell's next album, *Don Juan's Reckless Daughter*, which incorporated elements of jazz and Afro-Latin percussion, and the critics began labelling her music as folk-jazz.

In 1978 jazz bassist/composer Charles Mingus contacted Mitchell. He was dying of Lou Gehrig's disease and wanted her to collaborate with him on the final composition of his life. *Shadows And Light* followed in 1980, and *Wild Things Run Free*, released in 1982, has been hailed as her finest album since 1974's *Court And Spark.*

ELTON JOHN

Basically, the '70s produced fewer new and innovative acts than the previous decade, but one of the largest acts of the '70s was a man by the name of Reginald Dwight, better known as Elton John. John's enormous success in the '70s is remarkable in statistics alone—he had seven straight Number One albums, with four of them in the top 30 at the same time (a feat accomplished previously only by the Beatles).

Born in Middlesex, England, in 1947, John was hooked on music by the time he was old enough to listen to records. He started playing the piano at four, and by age 11 had earned a scholarship to the Royal Academy of Music. After discovering such rockers as Elvis Presley, Bill Haley, Little Richard and Jerry Lee Lewis, however, John realized he had found his niche and left the classics behind. At 14 he joined Bluesology, a small combo that backed the likes of Long John Baldry, Patti LaBelle, the Drifters and the Ink Spots. It was after quitting Bluesology, and deciding that Reg Dwight was not an appropriate name for a singer, that the name Elton John was created; Elton from Elton Dean, the band's sax player, and John from Long John Baldry.

Now on his own, John went to work for Dick James Music (the Beatles' early publishers), performing in demo sessions and composing music for lyrics sent in by an unknown writer named Bernie Taupin. Taupin and John eventually met, went for a cup of coffee, and the incredible duo that was to go on to create most of John's major hits was born.

When the contract with Dick James Music ran out, and after an unsuccessful attempt at recording other people's music, John and Taupin collaborated on their first album, *Empty Sky*, released in 1969. When the album did not fare well, arranger Paul Buckmaster and producer Gus Dudgeon were brought in to assist in the recording of the second album, *Elton John*, cut in 10 days. Although still not acclaimed in England, the album was a smash in the U.S. following the triumphant debut of John's performing talents at

One of the most innovative acts in the '7 was Elton John, who had seven straig number one selling albums, four of the in the top 30 at the same time. Elt announced his retirement several times the end of that decade, but he alwa came back for more and is still goi stron

Los Angeles' Troubadour and subsequent performances in New York and Philadelphia. By 1971 the second single, "Your Song," was on its way to becoming a pop standard.

Madman Across The Water (1971) had two moderate hits, "Levon" and "Tiny Dancer." However, the next two years were to prove to be John's most successful. *Honky Chateau* ('72), recorded in France, featured the hits "Rocket Man" and "Honky Cat." In January of 1973 *Don't Shoot Me, I'm The Piano Player* yielded the uptempo "Crocodile Rock" as well as the poignant "Daniel." Later that same year the double album set *Goodbye Yellow Brick Road* contained three smash hits, "Bennie And The Jets," "Saturday Night's Alright For Fighting" and the title song. In 1974 the album *Caribou* was released, containing two hits, "Don't Let The Sun Go Down On Me," and "The Bitch Is Back."

John pursued some other ventures such as his own record label and his performance as the Pinball Wizard in the film *Tommy* before recording *Captain Fantastic And The Brown Dirt Cowboy* ('75), a semiautobiographical album featuring the hit "Someone Saved My Life Tonight." 1975 also saw the release of *Rock Of The Westies* containing the successful "Island Girl." But the latter part of the '70s was a time of transition for John, who announced retirement several times, although he later returned with moderate success in the late '70s and in the early '80s with songs like "Little Jeannie," "Empty Garden" and "I'm Still Standing."

STEVIE WONDER

Stevie Wonder, né Steveland Morris, was born blind on May 13, 1950, in Saginaw, Michigan. He was playing the harmonica by age five, and at seven had mastered the piano after an old upright was given to him by a neighbor. At eight he learned to play drums on a set he received at a Christmas party for blind children.

In 1962, at age 12, he was introduced to Berry Gordy, Jr., at Motown Records, who dubbed him "Little Stevie Wonder" and signed him to a record contract. Wonder had his first hit in 1963 with "Fingertips—Part 2," which was a line recording featuring his proficiency on the harmonica. Wonder's career floundered for the next couple of years until the release in 1966 of *Uptight, Everything's Alright,* with the title song becoming a major hit. Again his career cooled somewhat throughout the end of the '60s, although he scored moderate hits with "I Was Made To Love Her," "For Once In My Life," "My Cherie Amour" and "Yester-Me, Yester-You, Yesterday." Finally, in 1970, after a battle with Motown for some artistic control, Wonder produced his own album *Signed, Sealed And Delivered*, with the title track becoming a major hit and including the single "We Can Work It Out," Wonder's R&B version of the Beatles' standard. Still not satisfied with his arrangement at Motown, however, Wonder left the label and became involved in producing other artists, only to return to Motown in 1972, garnering some unprecedented benefits like his own publishing and production companies as well as the largest monetary deal granted any artist of that time.

The first album after the renegotiation was only moderately successful; however the *Talking Book* album released in 1972 contained the smash hits "Superstition" and "You Are The Sunshine Of My Life." Wonder's next major hits, "Living For The City" and "Don't You Worry 'Bout A Thing" were on *Innervisions* ('73), on which Wonder played virtually all the instruments in addition to arranging and producing the album.

In 1974 Wonder retired from touring to work on his next release, a two-record set entitled *Songs In The Key Of Life* ('76). The collection of songs was a blend of many different types of material, from the upbeat "Sir Duke" and "I Wish" to the rhythmic "Another Star" and "As," to the pop "Isn't She Lovely."

Wonder spent the next three years on a movie soundtrack which was received poorly. He bounced back in the end of 1980 with the release of *Hotter Than July* and an instant smash hit entitled "Master Blaster (Jammin')."

THE JACKSON 5

With a father who played guitar and wrote music in his spare time and a mother who greatly enjoyed singing, it was only natural that the Jackson 5, five brothers of the nine children, would take up music. Sigmund Esco (Jackie), Toriano Adaryll (Tito), Jermaine LaJaune, Marlon David and Michael Joe began playing as a group and performing for their own pleasure in the late '60s. They become so well known in their hometown of Gary, Indiana, that in 1969 the mayor spoke about them to Diana Ross (of the Supremes), who was there doing a concert. She, in turn, took the news to Berry Gordy, Jr., of Motown Records, who followed up the lead and signed the group to a contract within a few weeks.

The band's first single, "I Want You Back" from the album of the same name, hit the top of the charts in January of 1969 when lead vocalist Michael, the youngest brother, was a mere 10 years old. Their incredible success continued when their second album, *ABC,* released in 1970, had a Number One hit with its title track. In the fall of the same year, their next album, simply called *Third Album,* produced the single "I'll Be There," which remained in the Number One position for five weeks and stayed in the top 10 for an amazing three months.

In 1971 the Jackson 5 kept up the same momentum. The hit single "Mama's Pearl" was followed by a ballad, "Never Can Say Goodbye," which sold 1,200,000 copies five days after its release, and late that year Motown began to push solo careers for Michael and Jermaine. Michael had three hit singles on his own in 1972, "Got To Be There," "Rockin' Robin" and a movie theme, "Ben." Jermaine also had a hit in 1973 with "Daddy's Home," the remake of the Shep and the Limelights' 1961 release.

Over the next few years the band had only moderate hits, and in 1976 they left Motown and moved to Epic Records. Changing their name to the Jacksons, they did not fare well until, in 1979, they began producing and writing their own material and scored a hit with "Shake Your Body."

Although in recent years the Jacksons have dropped considerably from the music scene, Michael, as a solo artist, has gone on to an incredible career. His first solo album, *Off The Wall* ('79), was a huge success and his release *Thriller* ('82) spawned three hits, "The Girl Is Mine," "Billie Jean," and "Beat It."

EARTH, WIND & FIRE

Probably the most commercial funk-R&B band to gain worldwide popularity, Earth, Wind & Fire crossed from the R&B charts into the pop charts, one of the few all-black groups to attain superstardom.

As a young man, leader Maurice White had entertained thoughts of teaching until 1963, when working as a session drummer at Chicago's Chess Records changed his life. After enjoying a stint with Ramsey Lewis, White moved to Los Angeles in 1970, where he formed Earth, Wind & Fire, obtaining a Warner Bros. recording contract. After two inauspicious albums, some changes in personnel were made and the group moved to Columbia Records. That label debut was *Last Days And Time,* released in 1972, followed by *Head To The Sky* the next year. "Evil" and "Keep Your Head To The Sky" both reached the top of the R&B charts. It was 1975, however, when EW&F made their landmark album *That's The Way Of The World,* their first to cross over into the pop charts. "Shining Star" won the group its first Grammy for best R&B single by a group, and the album reached the Number One position on the pop charts. Sellout concerts throughout the U.S. and Europe followed that year, and at the end of '75 the band released *Gratitude*, a two-record set, three sides of which were live. The album contained the Grammy award-winning "Can't Hide Love" and "Sing A Song."

1976 brought *Spirit,* yielding another hit, "Getaway," and the formation of White's Kalimba Productions. The next year *All In All* spawned two hit singles, "Serpentine Fire" and "Fantasy." *The Best Of Earth, Wind & Fire,* was also a smash, and "September," a previously unreleased tune, also reached the top of the charts. *I Am,* in 1979, included the smash hits "Boogie Wonderland" and "After The Love Is Gone," and that same year White established the American Recording Company, an actual record company, as an extension of his production company. In addition to EW&F, White signed Deniece Williams, the Emotions, Weather Report and D.J. Rogers to ARC.

The band's next big seller came in 1981 with *Raise,* which included the hit "Let's Groove," but the following year White, tired of extreme executive responsibilities, phased the record company out and reestablished his production company full force. In 1983, *Powerlight*'s first single, "Fall In Love With Me," reached the top of the charts. There seems to be no end to EW&F's magic.

THE COMMODORES

The Commodores, a six-piece, sometimes funky, sometimes sentimental band, hailed from the quiet town of Tuskegee, Alabama. The band was formed in 1967, and in 1968 two members were added, providing the lineup that would remain together for 15 years.

From their recording debut in 1974 on the Motown label, and their subsequent albums, the Commodores produced such hits as "Brick House," "Easy," "Sail On," "Three Times A Lady" and "Still," selling more than 40 million albums worldwide. As time went on, Lionel Richie, the band's lead vocalist and most prolific writer, wrote the hit "Lady" for Kenny Rogers, produced one of Rogers' albums, and wrote a movie theme song, "Endless Love," a duet he sang with Diana Ross. As he gained notoriety, Richie left the Commodores and has been enjoying a career as a solo artist with his first hit, the Grammy award-winning "Truly."

THE CARPENTERS

Perhaps the most successful brother-and-sister team to emerge in music was Karen and Richard Carpenter. In 1969, signed to A&M Records,

Above: By 1976 Michael McDonald had joined the Doobie Brothers, founded in the early '70s.

Below: The Bee Gees starred in the 1978 film *Sgt. Pepper's Lonely Hearts Club Band*.

their debut album, *Offering,* yielded a moderate hit with Lennon/McCartney's "Ticket To Ride." Album number two, *Close To You,* however, began a string of hits, first with the title tune, next with "We've Only Just Begun" and "For All We Know," followed by "Rainy Days And Mondays." Their fourth album, in 1971, spawned "Superstar," and the next year such hits as "Goodbye To Love," "It's Going To Take Some Time" and "Hurting Each Other." In 1973 "Yesterday Once More" reached the top of the charts, followed by "Top Of The World."

The duo faded from the public eye, but during the latter part of 1982 they were reportedly recording again and preparing to reemerge. On February 3, 1983, Karen Carpenter died of a massive cardiac arrest, a victim of anorexia nervosa.

STEELY DAN

Walter Becker and Donald Fagen formed Steely Dan in 1972, and with the distinction of being a popular band and not appearing live after a final 1974 tour, their studio albums were always anticipated and critically acclaimed. With a predominance of jazz combined with rock, their third album yielded their first major hit, "Rikki, Don't Lose That Number" ('74). It was three years before another smash, but *Aja* came up with three chart toppers, "Peg," "Deacon Blues" and "Josie." (The title track was in the film *FM.*) *Gaucho* in 1980 yielded a major hit with "Hey Nineteen," and 1982 produced a solo LP offering by Donald Fagen called *The Nightfly*.

THE DOOBIE BROTHERS

By the very early '70s the Doobie Brothers had established itself among the hippies and Hell's Angels of San Francisco. While their first album went unnoticed, by their second they had altered their personnel somewhat, becoming a two-guitar, two-drum outfit. Members included Pat Simmons, Tom Johnston, John Hartman, Tiran Porter (replacing Dave Shogren) and Mike Hossack. *Toulouse Street* ('72) hit with "Listen To The Music," followed by *The Captain And Me* which yielded "Long Train Runnin'" and "China Grove." Their biggest hit, however, occurred in 1974 with "Black Water" from their *What Were Once Vices Are Now Habits* album, and that same year Mike Hossack was replaced with Keith Knudsen, and Jeff Baxter officially became a member.

1975's *Stampede* featured "Take Me In Your Arms (Rock Me)" as their biggest hit, with two milder ones. That year, however, Tom Johnston took ill and Baxter called in Michael McDonald, a singer/songwriter/keyboardist, with whom he had worked in Steely Dan. With McDonald's arrival, the Doobie Brothers' commercial success escalated. While critics suggested that Pat Simmons' guitar rock and roll songs and McDonald's R&B-influenced keyboard tunes were too disparate, the musical marriage seemed to attract a broader audience and cement their popularity. Beginning with the Doobies' *Taking It To The Streets* album in 1976, McDonald wrote and/or sang most of the band's hits. They include the title song, followed by "Little Darling" (written by Holland-Dozier-Holland) from *Living On The Fault Line,* which also contained "You Belong To Me," a McDonald-Carly Simon collaboration. *Minute By Minute* brought several hits, including the title track, "Dependin' On You" and "What A Fool Believes" (a McDonald-Kenny Loggins collaboration) and also saw personnel changes, most notably Jeff Baxter's exit. Their final studio album in 1980, *One Step Closer,* offered hits with the title song and "Real Love," and in 1982 they embarked on their farewell tour. That same year saw the release of McDonald's first highly successful solo effort, and in the beginning of 1983 Simmons' first solo project was issued.

BEE GEES

The Bee Gees have enjoyed a most interesting and celebrated career. They actually began in the late '60s with such hits as "New York Mining Disaster—1941," "To Love Somebody," "Holiday," "Massachusetts," "Words," "I've Gotta Get A Message To You" and "I Started A Joke." They were one of the first popular groups to tour with a full orchestra, typical of their sound.

By 1970 the three Gibb brothers, Robin, Barry and Maurice, were left by their former accompanists, but hit with "Lonely Days" and "How Can You Mend A Broken Heart?" It wasn't until 1975, however, as disco began to gather momentum, that they had another two hits, "Jive Talkin'" and "Nights On Broadway." By the late '70s they had become known as the fathers of disco and their hits began to set precedents, including "You Should Be Dancing," "Love So Right," "I Just Want To Be Your Everything" and "(Love Is) Thicker Than Water." Composing nearly all of the soundtrack for the hit film *Saturday Night Fever* ('77), the Bee Gees scored with "How Deep Is Your Love," "Stayin' Alive" and "Night Fever," in addition to Yvonne Elliman's hit "If I Can't Have You." As well as writing a few hit songs for other artists, they continued to win with "Too Much Heaven," "Tragedy" and "Love You Inside Out" from their

Spirits Having Flown album ('79). Into the '80s, Barry Gibb produced and wrote songs for Barbra Streisand's *Guilty* albums and no doubt the Bee Gees will continue.

BARRY MANILOW

As one of the few '70s superstars, Barry Manilow holds the distinction of appealing to young and old alike. Although he is often criticized for his sentimental pop ballads, his success is inarguable.

While the house pianist at New York's famed Continental Baths, Manilow met up with Bette Midler in 1972. He co-produced and arranged the material for her first two albums, went on the road with her and stopped the show with his brief solo spot.

Manilow never intended to be a performer. He was interested in trying to sell his songs, arrangements and productions, but when he sang on the demo records he was offered a deal with Bell Records (now Arista). He decided to sign the contract, figuring it would be over after that first album anyway, but 10 years and a string of hits later Manilow is considered one of the finest entertainers in the business. From his 10 platinum-plus albums he has had such monster hits as "Mandy," "It's A Miracle," "Could It Be Magic," "I Write The Songs," "Tryin' To Get The Feeling," "This One's For You," "Weekend In New England," "Looks Like We Made It," "Daybreak," "Can't Smile Without You," "Even Now," "Copacabana," "Somewhere In The Night," "Ready To Take A Chance Again," "Ships," "When I Wanted You," "I Don't Wanna Walk Without You," "I Made It Through The Rain," "Lonely Together," "The Old Songs" and "Some Kind of Friend."

ROD STEWART

One of Rod Stewart's first gigs was with Long John Baldry in 1965. When that turned sour, Stewart ended up in a group with Mick Fleetwood called Shotgun Express, and when that band folded he was asked to join Jeff Beck as lead singer. After a tour of the U.S. with Beck, Stewart was offered a solo deal with Mercury Records. He signed the contract, but around the same time, in 1970, when Ron Wood was fired from Beck's group, Stewart quit as well. Both Wood and Stewart ended up in the mod group the Small Faces, and with their arrival the name changed to Faces. Finally, when Stewart's solo career became successful and Wood was asked to join the Rolling Stones, Faces disintegrated in 1975.

Stewart had recorded three albums by 1971 when he had his first hit single "Maggie May," and his albums *Every Picture Tells A Story* ('71) and *Never A Dull Moment* ('72) went gold (500,000 copies sold). When Stewart moved to Los Angeles at the end of the Faces in 1975, however, he released a couple of unsuccessful albums, bouncing back finally with single hits "Tonight's The Night," "The First Cut Is The Deepest" and "The Killing Of Georgie." 1977's *Foot Loose And Fancy Free* spun off a chart topper with "You're In My Heart," and in 1979 his disco song "Do Ya Think I'm Sexy" went to the top. "Ain't Love A Bitch" followed, with "Passion" hitting in 1980 and "Baby Jane" in 1983.

BRUCE SPRINGSTEEN

His nickname is "the Boss," just as Elvis Presley's was "the King." It is no wonder, since he has been hailed as the best rock and roll artist of the '70s.

Initially playing engagements in and around New Jersey, he came in contact with his future manager, Mike Appel. He was introduced to John Hammond, a Columbia executive who had signed the likes of Billie Holiday, Aretha Franklin and Bob Dylan, and Hammond signed Springsteen as well. In 1973, *Greetings From Asbury Park, New Jersey* was released, going fairly unnoticed. His second album later that year, *The Wild, The Innocent And The E-Street Shuffle*, also gathered little momentum, save building a sort of cult following and becoming a media favorite.

1975, however, proved both good and bad for Springsteen's career. His permanent back-up band, The E-Street Band, had been formed and *Born To Run* was released, catapulting its title track to the Number Three position on the charts. Springsteen, however, became a victim of media overkill, complete with overexposure and hype. His face appeared on the cover of both *Time* and *Newsweek,* and his sincerity was questioned when he was called "the next Bob Dylan" and "the savior of rock and roll." He then entered into a legal battle with manager Appel that kept him from recording for a year. Finally, *Darkness On The Edge Of Town* was released in 1978, but with no major hits. In the meanwhile, however, other artists were having hits with Springsteen compositions such as Manfred Mann's single "Blinded By The Night' ('77), Patti Smith's "Because The Night" ('78) and the Pointer Sisters' "Fire" ('79). By 1980 audiences and critics alike were eagerly anticipating the arrival of the album which had taken Springsteen a year to complete. *The River* was a major sensation and "Hungry Heart," one of the more commercial tunes, be-

came a chart topper. In 1981 he produced Gary U.S. Bonds' *Dedication* album, and in 1982 Springsteen released an acoustic album called *Nebraska,* recorded on a four-track without the backing of any musicians.

BILLY JOEL

Billy Joel's "Piano Man" was painfully autobiographical, written while playing bars in Los Angeles's San Fernando Valley. In 1973, after signing with Columbia Records, he released *Piano Man.* Ironically, the title tune became Joel's first hit. *Street Life Serenade,* the next year, spawned "The Entertainer," and *Turnstiles,* in 1976, contained two major hits for Joel, "New York State Of Mind" and "Say Goodbye To Hollywood."

In 1977 he attained major success with *The Stranger,* yielding the classic "Just The Way You Are," "Movin' Out (Anthony's Song)," "Only The Good Die Young" and "She's Always A Woman." *52nd Street* followed, including "My Life," "Big Shot," "Honesty" and "Until The Night." 1980's *Glass Houses* was met with continued success and offered the hits "You May Be Right," "It's Still Rock And Roll To Me" and "Don't Ask Me Why." In 1981 Columbia issued *Songs In The Attic,* a live rendition of selected songs from his past, and in 1982 *The Nylon Curtain* was released, including the hits "Allentown" and "Pressure" and carrying on the Joel tradition of telling it like it is.

KISS

Designed to appeal to young audiences as well as make money for the group members, Kiss came to life in 1973. The year before, Stanley Eisen, a.k.a. Paul Stanley, and Eugene Klein, a.k.a. Gene Simmons, had plotted out the venture, adding Paul "Ace" Frehley and Peter Criscoula (Criss). Utilizing the concept of theatrics and glitter Alice Cooper had employed, Kiss was the first act to be signed to Neil Bogart's Casablanca Records.

With masks of makeup disguising their true identities, the aura of mystery shrouding the band and its members served to popularize their heavy metal music. Without much airplay, Kiss albums still managed to go platinum (one million sold), and while they began to fade from the music scene by 1979, all members released solo albums simultaneously.

QUEEN

In 1971 Freddie Mercury, Brian May, John Deacon and Roger Taylor met while studying at various London colleges. Mercury had qualified for a diploma at Ealing College of Art, Taylor had trained as a dentist before switching to biology and earning a degree, Deacon obtained an honors degree in electronics and May had a BS in physics and experience as a teacher. There was a lot at stake when the four made a commitment to music. The first two years little happened, but in 1973 Elektra signed the band and "Keep Yourself Alive" and "Liar" from their debut album helped to establish them in the U.K. and the U.S. Their third album, *Sheer Heart Attack,* went into the top 10 and gave the band their first U.S. gold album. The release of *A Night At The Opera* was a turning point, and "Bohemian Rhapsody" became a worldwide hit. *A Day At The Races* ('76)

Kiss

From left: Freddie Mercury, John Deacon, Roger Taylor and Brian May came together in 1971 to form Queen, and although they were extremely successful, they didn't have a Number One hit until "We Are The Champions" in 1977.

was their first self-produced album and yielded another smash single, "Somebody To Love." *News Of The World* in 1977 had their first Number One hit, "We Are The Champions," after which the band decided to manage themselves and have done so ever since. Their seventh album, *Jazz,* contained "Bicycle Race" and their 1978 tour yielded *Live Killers.* In 1979 Queen recorded a few singles which were later included on *The Game.* "Crazy Little Thing Called Love" was their biggest chart success, going to the top in the U.S., Mexico, Canada, Australia, Israel, Holland and Belgium. "Save Me" followed with good response, and "Another One Bites The Dust," the third single from *The Game,* went to the top of pop *and* soul charts in America. Next, the band accepted an offer from Dino DeLaurentiis to score the film *Flash Gordon.* In 1981 Roger Taylor's solo album, *Fun In Space,* was released. Queen's *Hot Space,* in an R&B vein, was released the following year and was not met with the usual success, but most likely they will return to their original format by the next release.

STYX

One of the biggest concert draws today, Styx made an inauspicious debut on Wooden Nickel Records, a regional (Chicago) RCA affiliate. Dennis De Young, Chuck and John Panozzo and James Young had already been together for several years by the time *Styx 1* was released in 1970. *Styx 2* yielded the hit "Lady," but, after several albums for Wooden Nickel, Styx moved on to bigger and better things with A&M in 1975. Their first album for that label, *Equinox,* had the hit "Lorelei," after which Tommy Shaw joined in time for the recording of their next album, *Crystal Ball.*

Grand Illusion, actually the band's seventh album, was their major breakthrough, beginning the unbreakable string of platinum-selling albums. "Come Sail Away" was a major hit, and their *Cornerstone* LP included their smash "Babe." *Paradise Theatre* in 1981 was hailed as their best album, and their 1983 release, *Kilroy Was Here,* proved to be another successful concept album.

FOREIGNER

In 1977 Foreigner's debut album sold nearly four million copies during its two-year run on national charts. With three hit singles, "Feels Like The First Time," "Cold As Ice" and "Long, Long Way From Home," the band began an extremely successful career.

The band came together the year before when Mick Jones (ex-Spooky Tooth) and Ian McDonald (ex-King Crimson) met up and recruited Al Greenwood, Lou Gramm, Ed Gagliardi and Dennis Elliot. Determined to be a live group, they practiced for months before setting out to record their first album. Their second album, *Double Vision,* included hits with the title track, "Hot Blood" and "Blue Morning, Blue Day."

Before their *Head Games* album, Gagliardi was replaced with Rick Wills, and after their big hit "Dirty White Boy," founder McDonald and Greenwood left the band, leaving the group a quartet. Their fourth album, entitled simply *4* ('81), was the first to make it to the Number One chart position, with two singles from it, "Urgent" and "Waiting For A Girl Like You," proving successful. Their fifth album, *Records,* was released early in 1983.

The 1978 version of Journey included Gregg Rolie, who was replaced by Jonathan Cain.

The Journey lineup: (From left) Ross Valory, Neal Schon, Steve Perry, Steve Smith and Jonathan Cain.

CHAPTER ELEVEN

JOURNEY

Many people do not realize that Journey, perhaps the most popular band of the last few years, is now in its 11th year and *Frontiers* marks its 10th album (including the live *Captured* and *In The Beginning,* a compilation album of their first three releases).

As Journey bassist Ross Valory puts it, "There have been many changes through the years, a lot of heartaches, struggles and a lot of people who have come and gone in the band, as well as the organization itself."

As the head of the organization (called Nightmare, their perception of the business when they entered it) is manager Walter "Herbie" Herbert, a man group members greatly respect.

"I always had the feeling that the success was possible," Valory states. "I never doubted we could do it and that we had the right components and the right approach. A lot of it, though, had to do with my belief in Herbie as a manager and mentor, and his ability to persevere and continue to grow. As much as a band can do with talent, the other half is so important. There are so many bands you know of that have talent and the right thing, but what happened? How come they're not coming across? It's usually because of management."

Herbert brought the initial core members together in 1973. In 1966 he had managed a San Francisco band called Frumious Bandersnatch which included Valory on bass, and when that group ceased he worked as a production manager for the then fledgling Santana. That band initially contained Gregg Rolie, and later a 15-year-old Neal Schon. Through his friendship with Herbert, Valory met Rolie and Schon and Herbert reintroduced them when Valory departed Steve Miller's band at approximately the same time as Schon and Rolie left Santana. They asked Prairie Prince (of the Tubes) to assist on drums and added rhythm guitarist George Tickner to complete the outfit.

"The musical experience was magical," Valory recalls. "It moved very quickly and magically for a group of people who had really never played together before. It was very spontaneous. At that time the musical direction was more experimental and instrumentally oriented. Basically we were just playing what we wanted to play without necessarily anything else in mind as far as audience, image or direction. A month after we began rehearsing, we recorded our material on a demonstration tape [most of which, in fact, did end up on their self-titled debut album] but then we got in a jam with not being able to maintain Prairie's involvement. Thus began the great drummer hunt."

They found Aynsley Dunbar just as he had completed his work with David Bowie, and Dunbar joined in February 1974. *Journey* was released in 1975, George Tickner left, and the struggle for attention began. The band came in through the back door, so to speak, establishing itself through live performance. For the first few years the road work provided their bread and butter since they were on tour for 11 months out of the year.

Current member Steve Smith explains the situation: "There are three ways of making it—touring, airplay and the combination. When Supertramp was selling more records than we were, with *Breakfast In America* which sold four million records, they couldn't play the same places we were playing when we were selling a million records."

FM radio aided the cause somewhat by giving their albums *Look Into The Future* ('76) and *Next* ('77) some airplay, but the records sold approximately 100,000 each. Since an opening act makes little more than enough money to pay expenses and break even, Gregg Rolie generously helped the band financially for a period of time from monies earned from the more lucrative Santana days. But the record company, CBS, stuck by them, backing their projects because it saw potential.

By 1977 the band began to contemplate a radical change in format. They realized that neither Rolie nor Schon was lead singer material, so they added vocalist Robert Fleischman for *Next* and also realized they had gone as far as they could with their then song structure.

"We got to the point where we couldn't extend ourselves further in an instrumental way," Rolie admits. "We began to write differently, more lyrically oriented and toward the vocal process. In that process Steve Perry arrived, actually in the mail through a tape to Herbie."

Prior to Journey, Steve Perry had been involved in a couple of Los Angeles groups, one called Pieces, with Tim Bogert, and another called the Alien Project. The Alien Project had been preparing to record for its newly signed label, CBS, when the bass player-singer was killed suddenly in an auto accident. CBS then suggested Perry send a tape to Journey and they grabbed him. With Fleishman out and Perry in, the turning point album, *Infinity*, was recorded.

Although *Infinity* became a platinum seller and got some AM airplay with "Wheel In The Sky" and "Lights," it was not a substantial improvement. To radio stations, Journey was still not a proven entity. Once again, however, Herbert put his business sense to work.

"With the release of *Infinity*, the band went from an opening act to a headliner, even though, for all practical purposes, it wasn't ready. Herbie made it look like Journey was ready by booking a tour where the band headlined," Smith explains.

Jonathan Cain

Ross Valory

Neal Schon

Steve Perry

The new format, though, did upset some fans, who were even abusive to newcomer Perry. They performed half old and half new material and didn't bring Perry on until the third tune, but to many fans the change was still radical. In proportion to the number of fans they accumulated on that grand tour, however, the loss didn't matter.

That tour was also where members first came in contact with Smith, who was in one of the opening acts, Montrose. In 1978, Dunbar, who Valory described as one of the finest soloists in the world, was replaced by Smith, said to be more of a team player.

"He (Dunbar) did a gallant job in the *Infinity* project, restraining and holding down to the basics for the sake of the melody and the way it was orchestrated. I think he may have found it very frustrating as a player's player," Valory says.

Indeed. Dunbar's distaste for the unit grew as they became less experimental and more formatted. "The beginning of Journey was a real player's paradise," says Dunbar, "but after you had learned the songs, they wanted them to be played the same every night, which doesn't do very much for playing. The excitement for me is in stretching out and being able to play, but they didn't want that."

According to Dunbar, they fired him "out of the blue," causing him to begin a bitter lawsuit. Shortly thereafter Dunbar became the Jefferson Starship's drummer until 1982.

By virture of his background, Steve Smith seemed an odd choice to fill Dunbar's seat in Journey. Groomed by the Berklee School of Music, Smith's jazz roots were audible with Jean Luc-Ponty and Montrose, but Smith argues, "Music is still music. It's not like we all came from different backgrounds and we forget those background to play something different. It's because we all come from different backgrounds that we sound the way we do."

Smith's powerhouse drumming on *Evolution*, however, helped complete the new direction. The album not only went platinum, but they gained a substantial increase of airplay with their first top-20 single, "Lovin,' Touchin', Squeezin.' "

While the band recorded its sixth Columbia release, *Departure*, a double-record set, *In The Beginning*, was released, comprised of the best material from the first three albums. By 1981, however, Gregg Rolie departed and Journey's release, *Escape*, clinched their superstardom. With the arrival of Jonathan Cain (ex-Babys member) the previous year, Steve Perry found the perfect writing partner and the two collaborated on the monster hits "Who's Crying Now" and "Open Arms," as well as "Don't Stop Believin' " and "Still They Ride" (the latter two with Neal Schon). It seems that with the precedent set by *Escape*, the band can do no wrong. 1983's *Frontiers* went quickly to the top of the charts, as well as their first single release, "Separate Ways (Worlds Apart)," followed by "Faithfully."

But the price of mass success is high when it comes to critics. In the early days Journey garnered favorable reviews as the underdogs; but as soon as they became platinum sellers, hence commercially accepted, the battle with the press began. In late 1982 they took yet another step for which they received critical barbs. They were the first group to have a video game produced in their name, and despite the criticism it started a trend; and many groups have followed suit.

"Some people aren't into the concept of band and business. We're artists, but if there can be money made on the business side of it, why not?" Smith asks. "Obviously we did the game to make money. We're not doing it because we wanted to make a state-of-the-art video game. That wasn't our intent, although we tried to make the best game we could. And it really is a good game. It uses 100% of its memory and it's not like any other game. But if people didn't want it, they wouldn't buy it. If they like it, great."

Now that their tour schedule has decreased to only some five or six months out of the year, each member has time to pursue his own special interest in addition to band responsibilities. Neal Schon has collaborated on two projects with Jan Hammer and will be doing a project with Sammy Hagar as well, while Steve Smith has worked with keyboardist Tom Coster on some projects, and his first solo jazz album was released during the summer of '83. Steve Perry will begin work on a solo project in the fall of 1983, Jonathan Cain is assisting his wife Tane's musical career, and Ross Valory plans to put his video madness to work on some documentaries.

Journey's future also includes video and they are expected to do a video of an entire future album. "We're going to continue what we're doing and grow as players, writers and performers. We want to grow sonically in the quality of our records so that we make state-of-the-art records," Smith projects for the future.

"Our new frontiers are conquering Europe now and making it Down Under (Australia)," Valory adds. "We're finally getting quite a bit of attention in Britain, which is a real hard nut to crack. I mean, after all, there was a time when we talked about the East Coast as the foreign market."

"Heart of Glass" was Blondie's first hit in the United States though the group, with some personnel changes, had been around since 1975.

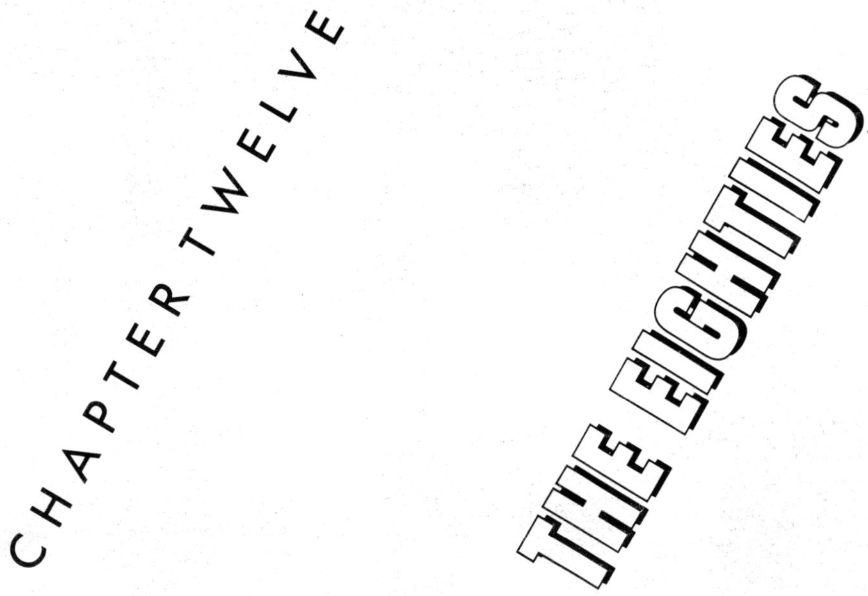

CHAPTER TWELVE

THE EIGHTIES

Perhaps a reaction to the mild tempered, uninspiring music of the '70s was the radical punk music that began in England in the late '70s or the driving, less violent new-wave movement. In 1975 the Sex Pistols' "Anarchy In The U.K." embodied punk with its typical rage. As the Sex Pistols were on their way out, however, the Clash was on its way in. More political and less destructive than the Pistols, their energy was channeled differently and audiences and critics hailed them as the answer to the lost dream of the Beatles.

Small groups sprang up everywhere, reminiscent of the '60s. The major difference was that, while most record companies jumped on the bandwagon, chances just weren't being taken as in the days post-Beatles. The economy was in a different state, and while the music was different, it was not the complete change that had occurred in the '60s. Record company executives pondered its longevity and it is really still too early to predict the impact of punk and new wave, its durability and its staying power.

Rock and roll, heavy metal and pop-rock are still forms very much alive, and those bands, along with those innovative new-wave bands who have remained on the scene with ongoing success, are the subjects of this chapter.

BLONDIE

Members Debbie Harry, Chris Stein, Gary Valentine, James Destri and Clem Burke got together in 1975 and independently recorded their first single, "X Offender(s)." Private Stock Records signed the band and their first self-titled album was released the following year. Before their second album, however, Gary Valentine departed and Nigel Harrison and Frank Infante joined. While *Plastic Letters* was recorded in the summer of 1977, it was not released until 1978, for halfway through their recording they bought out of Private Stock to sign with Chrysalis. *Parallel Lines*, also released that year, was the first album to go platinum, and "Heart Of Glass" went to the top in the U.S. With their fourth album, *Eat To The Beat,* Blondie had the distinction of being the first band to simultaneously release a full-length video and album, which included the hit single "Dreaming."

Among other independent activities, Debbie Harry collaborated in 1980 with Giorgio Moroder on "Call Me," the title track from *American*

Gigolo, which stayed at Number One for four weeks. She has also acted in such films as *Union City* and *Roadie*, in addition to releasing a solo album, *Koo-Koo*.

In the summer of 1980 Blondie's *Autoamerican* was recorded, containing the singles, "The Tide Is High" and "Rapture." In 1982 the band released its sixth album, *The Hunter*.

THE PRETENDERS

After a lot of maybes and almosts, Chrissie Hynde got a phone call about one of her original compositions, "The Phone Call." Real Records was interested and Hynde set about to form a band. Through a mutual friend, Chrissie was introduced to Pete Farndon, James Honeyman-Scott and James Mcleduff. They cut "Stop Your Sobbing," which Nick Lowe produced, and unhappy with Mcleduff as drummer, brought in Martin Chambers. He had played with Honeyman-Scott previously and knew Farndon, for all three were from Hereford, England, a town where there was little to do besides be in a band. The three had auditioned countless drummers, but when Chambers sat down with them, they knew the magical chemistry had been completed. The day they asked Chambers to join, Chrissie cut his hair for the photographs for the cover of "Stop Your Sobbing." The single entered the top 30 and they were on their way. "Kid," penned by Hynde, reached the top 30 and their third single, "Brass In Pocket," went to Number Five. Incredibly enough, their debut album, produced by Chris Thomas, entered the British charts at Number One in 1980.

While the Pretenders were in America, "Brass In Pocket" was doing quite well, and back in England "Talk Of The Town" began to make its mark. By November of that year the band began working on their second album in Paris, and the first release, early in 1981, "Message Of Love," hit. *Pretenders II* was finally released in July of that year, but on June 17, 1982, James Honeyman-Scott died at age 25. With Farndon (who died in April of 1983) exiting as well, two new members, Malcolm Foster and Robbie McIntosh, were invited into the group early in 1983, and their first single, "Back On The Chain Gang," became a chart topper.

PAT BENATAR

Pat Benatar, ne Pat Andrzejewski, another dynamo female vocalist, hit stardom in 1980. She was discovered at a talent showcase club, Catch A Rising Star, by its owner, Rick Newman, who became her manager. In 1979 she landed a recording contract and it wasn't long before her debut album, *In The Heat Of The Night*, spawned two top-30 singles, "Heartbreaker" and "We Live For Love."

Her music was mistakenly labeled as new-wave for a time. In actuality, Benatar's classically trained voice was doing nothing more than belting good old rock and roll. Her second album, *Crimes Of Passion*, yielded "Hit Me With Your Best Shot" and "Treat Me Right," after which she married her guitarist Neil Geraldo and she and her band took a year's break before working on their *Get Nervous* LP, from which "Shadows Of The Night" headed to the top of the charts.

THE POLICE

One of the most innovative groups of the new wave genre, blending reggae and rock, drummer Stewart Copeland organized the Police in London in 1977. He persuaded Sting to leave his teaching job and recruited Henri Padovani on guitar, and the trio recorded a homemade single called "Fall Out." Later that year Copeland and Sting ventured to France to work on a musical project called Strontium 90, in which they first played with guitarist Andy Summers. Andy joined the force and when they returned to England Padovani left the group. Once more a trio, with the help of Stewart's brother-turned-manager, Miles, they played scattered clubs and it was in 1978 that A&M Records cautiously agreed to sign the Police to a singles deal. When "Roxanne" hit, they were asked to sign an album deal.

Outlandos d' Amour, their debut album, included the hit "Roxanne," and *Regatta de Blanc*, their second LP, contained "Message In A Bottle" and "Walking On The Moon." *Zenyatta Mondatta* ('80), had two monster hits, "De Do Do Do, De Da Da Da" and "Don't Stand So Close To Me." Their fourth highly successful release, *Ghosts In The Machine*, contained the smash hits "Every Little Thing She Does Is Magic" and "Spirits In The Material World." *Synchronicity*, released in the summer of 1983 and containing "Every Breath You Take," promises to be their biggest album yet.

All three individuals have pursued outside projects as well, with Copeland releasing product under the pseudonym of Klark Kent and scoring a Francis Ford Coppola film, Sting acting in a variety of films (including a role in The Who's *Quadrophenia*) and Andy Summers doing a collaborative effort with Robert Fripp.

THE CARS

The first American group to infiltrate with a commercialized version of the new English sound

was the Cars. The group began when Ric Ocasek and Benjamin Orr met at a party in 1972. After playing Boston clubs as a duo, the two met Greg Hawkes and formed a trio called Richard and the Rabbits. Hawkes left, however, to join Martin Mull's group, Fabulous Furniture, and Ocasek and Orr resumed their duo format. In 1976 the duo met Elliot Easton and formed Cap'n Swing, adding David Robinson. In January 1977, Hawkes returned to complete the five-man lineup. Shortly thereafter they cut their first demo while establishing themselves as Boston's top new group.

In December Elektra signed the band, "Just What I Needed," their first single from their debut album, did well, and the Cars were hailed as the most innovative band of their time. After three successful singles from their first album, they were named the Best New Artist of 1978 by readers of *Rolling Stone*, *Creem*, *Crawdaddy*, *Circus* and *Performance* magazines, and the album went up to Number Eight on the charts. In June of 1979 *Candy-O* went to 48 a week after its release, with "Let's Go" reaching Number Three. "Touch And Go" from their 1980 album *Panorama* went top 40, and their fourth-album, *Shake It Up*, was their fastest-breaking album, as was the single of the same name.

In 1982 leader Ric Ocasek, always involved in such outside projects as producing other artists, released his first solo album, *Beatitude*.

THE GO-GO'S

Holding the distinction of being the most popular all-female band of our time, the original lineup (Margot Oliverra, Elissa Bello, Jane Wiedlin and Belinda Carlisle) got together in 1978. Just a few months later Charlotte Caffey was added and a year later Gina Schock replaced Bello.

Taking the surf music of the '50s and new wave of the '80s, the combined elements were heard on their first record, "We Got The Beat" for Still Records, and all those subsequent recordings. At the end of 1980 Oliverra was replaced by Kathy Valentine, and soon after they recorded their first album on IRS (label of Miles Copeland, brother of The Police's Stewart Copeland). Released in July 1981, by March of the next year, it had reached the Number One position on the charts.

Managing to win over audiences and critics alike, the Go-Go's have dispelled the stereotype that women can't attain and maintain success in the music industry. Their follow-up album, *Vacation* ('82), was also highly successful and critically acclaimed, indicating their first-time-around success was no fluke.

TOTO

Toto is a force to be reckoned with in the '80s. At the 1982-83 Grammy Awards, it was a near clear sweep for the band and its fourth album.

The band was formed in 1978 of seasoned session musicians who have recorded for the likes of Paul McCartney, Boz Scaggs, Michael Jackson, Aretha Franklin, Steely Dan, Barbra Streisand and an endless list. In fact, members David Paich, Jeff Porcaro, Steve Porcaro, Steve Lukather, Bobby Kimball and David Hungate (replaced by Mike Porcaro in 1982) have had a lot of journalistic flak for the fact that they were primarily known as session players and perhaps were too polished to maintain the energy of a garage band.

They did, however, start out as a garage band. As youngsters, David Paich and Jeff Porcaro were introduced through their music industry fathers (Marty Paich and Joe Porcaro) and played with one another. The studio work was spurred by a road gig with Sonny & Cher as 17-year-old boys. Saving money, working sessions, they finally activated their dream of putting a band together and signed with Columbia Records. Their debut album, *Toto*, spawned a smash hit, "Hold The Line" and a couple of other moderate hits. *Hydra* managed the hit "99" and *Turn Back* did not fare as successfully. 1982, however, brought *Toto IV* and the sensational "Rosanna," followed by "Make Believe," "Africa" and "I Won't Hold You Back."

RICK SPRINGFIELD

Actually, Rick Springfield is enjoying his second shot of success in the '80s. Certainly he did not go as far the first time around, but in 1972 he had a big hit with "Speak To The Sky." The Australian import was extremely unhappy, however, when he was marketed as a teen idol, and he bailed out of his management and recording contracts. Tied up in litigation for a while, it wasn't until 1980 that Springfield signed with RCA.

Just as his first album, *Working Class Dog*, was released, he landed a role on one of daytime TV's most popular soap operas, *General Hospital*. His album skyrocketed to the top of the charts, as well as the first single, "Jessie's Girl," followed by "I've Done Everything For You." *Success Hasn't Spoiled Me Yet*, his follow-up release, also was a smash success, spawning "Don't Talk To Strangers" and "What Kind Of Fool Am I."

Exiting *General Hospital*, Springfield was able to concentrate on his top priority, music. 1983's release, *Living In Oz*, marks a maturation in his writing, and he's completed his first role in a major motion picture, *Hard To Hold*.

The Go-Go's

STRAY CATS

Although their genuine affection for the style and flash of '50s rockola and the emphasis they placed on trying to recapture the wild and raw spirit of the original rock 'n' rollers brought them a following in New York where they had their origins, the Stray Cats were a relatively unknown group until they headed to the U.K. in 1980 to search for the young rocker rebels in London who might tune into their sound. Their fortune took a turn for the better after a chance meeting with the original Police and Electric Chairs guitarist Henri Padovani, who introduced them to Claudine Riley, a publicist working for press agent Keith Altam (The Who, Rolling Stones), who managed to get the unknown group booked into clubs. It took only a few shows to spread the word. The sheer vitality of the Cats' stage performance, welded with the spirit of old-time rock combined with the musical toughness and visual punch of the '80s, soon made them the talk of the town. Their reputation blossomed enough for Rolling Stones' Mick Jagger, Keith Richards and Charlie Watts to check out a performance. The Rolling Stones members were so taken with the group they offered them an opening spot on part of their 1981 tour of the United States.

The three musicians behind the Stray Cats phenomenon are 23-year-old guitarist Brian Setzer, 21-year-old bassist Lee Rocker and 21-year-old drummer Slim Jim Phantom. Their two English albums, *Stray Cats* (rated the Number One LP of the year by British critics when released), and *Gonna Ball*, went to the top of the charts in England, but American audiences had to wait until the Cats released *Built For Speed* in 1983 in American to latch onto the group's sound. The LP's title track was written specifically for the album (which contains the choice material from the two English LPs), and bristles with the intensity of the pioneer rock 'n' rollers who inspired it—Gene Vincent, Eddie Cochran, Elvis Presley and Johnny Burnette. The LP spawned two hit singles, "Stray Cat Strut" and "Rock This Town," and their next album *Rant And Rave* proved the Cats really were *Built For Speed*—and staying power!